TROUBLE RISING
By Emme Rollins

Ernst Fraenkel

FIDO publishing

Trouble Rising © 2016 by Emme Rollins

All rights reserved under the International and Pan-American Copyright Conventions. No part of this book may be reproduced or transmitted in any form or by any means, electronic or mechanical, including photocopying, recording, or by any information storage and retrieval system, without permission in writing from the publisher.

This is a work of fiction. Names, places, characters and incidents are either the product of the author's imagination or are used fictitiously, and any resemblance to any actual persons, living or dead, organizations, events or locales is entirely coincidental.

FIDO Publishing, LLC
486 S Ripley #164
Alpena MI 49707

To order additional copies of this book, contact:
books@fidopublishing.com
www.fidopublishing.com

Cover Art © Taria Reed 2015

Warning: the unauthorized reproduction or distribution of this copyrighted work is illegal. Criminal copyright infringement, including infringement without monetary gain, is investigated by the FBI and is punishable by up to 5 years in prison and a fine of $250,000.

Chapter One

I guess I shouldn't have been surprised to find out that Trouble was breaking up in *Variety*, but somehow, it surprised me anyway.

I sat there, staring at the words, with the sinking realization that when it came to Tyler and his secrets, I seemed to always be the last one to know. Then I saw the byline.

Alisha McKenna.

I should have known.

The little redhead with the great big green eyes and the great big silicone tits who had been begging for an interview from Tyler since before we were even married. He'd always been partial to redheads, hadn't he? I remember, the roadies said something snide about that once. So what had made Tyler finally grant Alisha McKenna an interview?

Not just an interview, I thought, blinking at the headline—*Trouble's in Trouble: Is The Ultimate Boy Band Breaking Up?*—but the scoop of the goddamned century. At least in the entertainment world. This wasn't just news. This was a front-page, oh-em-gee, did-you-hear, mind-blowing story that was about to send every girl from the ages of twelve to twenty-something into palsied fits of downright insanity.

Including me.

Trouble's breaking up?

I mean, I knew, probably more than anyone else, that Trouble was in trouble. Tyler was exhausted, trying to keep up with the band and taping the *Album* series on top of it. He'd won two Emmys for the show on HBO—the critics loved it and the fans loved it even more. For the first time since Trouble's inception, lead guitarist Tyler Cook had surpassed lead singer Rob Burn's popularity in teen 'zine polls.

My husband had finally become a true teen heartthrob, instead of just "the other cute one" in Trouble—the number one rock-slash-pop-slash-boy-band, depending on who you asked. Tyler's brother, lead singer Rob Burns, had always been the front man, the center of attention, the one in the spotlight. Now Tyler was giving him a run for his money, a fact Rob claimed he didn't mind, although secretly, I think he did, at least a little bit.

But if Tyler left the band, Rob wouldn't have to worry about his younger brother hogging the spotlight anymore, would he?

It wasn't like Tyler hadn't talked about it. We'd had long, heartfelt conversations into the night about Tyler leaving Trouble, the pros and cons, all the implications and ramifications, from big to small and back again. We'd tossed it like a ball, back and forth between us, a game of hot potato, neither of us wanting to be left holding a decision that would affect not only our lives, but everyone we knew.

Apparently, Tyler had finally decided to decide.
Without me.

I couldn't believe it. But it was true. The headline glared back at me, defiant, black and white. Tyler had told Alisha McKenna what he'd decided to do. Alisha-*bottomless-cleavage*-McKenna. He'd called and she'd printed. I was left entirely out of the loop.

- 2 -

My phone buzzed on the table and I turned it over to see Sabrina's name come up on the display. Had my best friend in the world read the article? Of course she had. And she was calling to find out if I'd known. That would be the first question out of her mouth—*Katie, did you know about this? What's going on?* And what would I say? What could I say.

I had no idea.

I'm his goddamned wife, and I had no idea.

Well, that wasn't entirely true. I'd known it was a possibility, some day. That Tyler was tired, that his hands, his poor hands, were just going to get worse due to the rheumatoid arthritis he'd been diagnosed with when he was just a teen—a disease he refused to tell anyone about. Except me.

Granted, a new medication, plus a radical change in his diet, seemed to have stemmed the decline, but age would only make it worse. Eventually, he just wouldn't be able to play guitar anymore, no matter how much pain medication he took. Besides, HBO had renewed *Album*—it had surpassed *Game of Thrones* in ratings during its second season—and Tyler was the star.

The phone buzzed in my hand and I looked at Sabrina's name, debating whether or not I wanted to take the call. What was I supposed to tell her? *Well, I knew he was kind of thinking about it, but I had no idea he'd made a decision...*

I couldn't believe he'd decided without me.

I tossed the phone back on the table, finishing my coffee in two big gulps. It was still too hot and I burned my tongue, but I didn't care. I folded the paper so the headline was prominent, putting it on the kitchen table next to my empty cup. Then I turned the ringer off on my phone and waited for Tyler get back from his morning swim.

The ocean was right outside our back door, and he swam in it every chance he got. Rob and Sabrina had a giant pool, but we preferred the thunder of the ocean. Swimming in it was an experience. There was always a slight hint of danger in it, unlike the placid experience of a pool.

I suppose it was a pretty apt metaphor for our lives, the four of us. Rob and Sabrina were pool people. Calm, clean, warm water. No waves. Nothing to disrupt the placid surface. Me and Tyler? We were definitely ocean sorts. Jagged rocks, jellyfish, even sharks. Bring it on.

I got up to raid the fridge while I waited for my husband to return from his morning swim. Rob and Sabrina had a cook, a driver, a housekeeper, but we'd never gotten around to employing any of those, in spite of the giant size of the house. We liked our privacy—mostly the ability to be able to have sex in every room in the house whenever we wanted.

We did have a couple housekeepers—but no one live-in. They came a few times a week, cleaning all the rooms on a rotation. I couldn't have cleaned this whole house by myself, no way.

And we did subscribe to a food service that delivered fresh, organic food to our fridge for the weekdays. We cooked together as much as we possibly could, depending on Tyler's schedule. Given Tyler's condition, I was determined to keep him on the diet that had proven effective in decreasing general inflammation and easing his pain.

But oh God, did I miss junk food. So I kept a stash, hidden away where Tyler couldn't find it and ate it when he wasn't around. And right now, I needed a goddamned York Peppermint Patty. I hid them in a freezer-burned bag of Okra at the back of the freezer. The slit in the middle had been opened and resealed with Scotch tape. Tyler would never in a million years think to look there.

Frozen Peppermint Patties were one of my favorites—like little mouth orgasms. I let the chocolate melt on my tongue, wishing the sweet, brightness of it could wash away the bitterness I was feeling.

Here I thought we were doing so well, me and Tyler. We'd only been married a few years, but that was like twenty-something in Hollywood years. The tabloids and TMZ constantly photographed us as a couple, speculating on how long it would last, and Tyler and I would read the articles and laugh.

Because we were invincible. We were going to be like Kurt Russell and Goldie Hawn, or Susan Sarandon and Tim Robbins. Before they broke up, anyway. But you know, one of those couples who last and last, for twenty or thirty years—which worked out to just about forever in Hollywood years.

And we were going to last forever, because we were just that much in love. I told Tyler everything, good or bad, and he did the same with me. *No more secrets* had been our mantra since we'd decided to get married. There had been plenty of them before that, but none since.

Except now, there was.

I took another Peppermint Patty out, resealing the bag and shoving it to the back of the freezer behind the frozen steaks and pork roast—all grass-fed and hormone free, of course—where I knew Tyler would never look. Besides, he hated Peppermint Patties. If they'd been Snickers or Kit-Kats, he would have devoured them, but even if he found my secret stash, he'd probably turn his nose up at it.

I drifted across the kitchen to look out the back doors—a wall of sliding glass, really—to look for Tyler. I saw his head bobbing in the waves, and the sight of his dirty-blonde hair slicked back, his skin tawny from the sun, made me smile in spite of the anger bubbling in my chest.

It was hard for me to stay mad at Tyler.

But he lied to you.

The headline was still glaring at me from the table, along with Alisha-*I'm-an-obvious-whore-*McKenna's byline.

Secrets. God, I hated secrets.

Like your secret stash?

"Oh come on," I muttered, shaking my head with a snort. It wasn't as if my secret stash of junk food was in any way comparable to Tyler telling a reporter he was leaving Trouble before he told me. Or his brother. Or the band.

And my secret was just a little white lie. It was for his own good, after all. *So maybe he thought doing it this way was for everyone's good?*

I snorted again at that, seeing Tyler wading toward the shore. He was like a Greek god coming out of the surf, a reverse Venus, so beautiful it was almost blinding. And he was mine. All mine. To hell with Alisha-*call-me-anytime-Tyler*-McKenna. She wasn't the one who had him in her bed every night, was she? So she'd gotten him to tell her he was thinking about leaving Trouble. She'd probably tricked him into it.

Or maybe he didn't really tell her at all.

That possibility occurred to me, a bright flash through the red haze of my anger. What if Alisha-*I'll-do-anything-for-a-scoop*-McKenna had made it up? It wouldn't be the first time someone in the press had misconstrued something Tyler said, or just outright made something up and lied about it. The tabloids could take one tiny bit of truth and twist it to fit whatever story they wanted to tell.

So give him the benefit of the doubt.

Okay, I could do that much, I decided, taking my seat again at our kitchen table. It was really more of a breakfast nook, cozy and sweet, brightly lit in the morning, a definite selling point when we bought the house.

I slid onto the bench seat, checking my phone—I'd silenced the ringer, but when I flipped it over, I saw a bunch of texts and calls had come in since that first call from Sabrina. Everyone had read the article, apparently. Even Rob had called me.

Tyler came in the back door, dripping wet, a towel draped around his shoulders. He shook off like a wet dog, then toweled his hair dry, smiling as he padded barefoot across the marble floor toward me. He stopped at the coffee maker to pour himself a cup, bringing the pot over to the table.

"Good swim?" I watched him pour more coffee into my cup.

"Great." He leaned over to kiss the top of my head, hearing him breathe me in. I smiled when he dipped lower to nuzzle my ear, sending little electrical shivers down my arm to tingle my fingertips. "Not as good as you this morning, though... I didn't want to get out of bed."

"Me either," I confessed, feeling that strong, steady pulse between my thighs that being around Tyler always elicited. I still wanted him just as much as the first time we'd met. "But I promised Sabrina I'd meet her for lunch. And don't you have the read-through? For the show?"

"Rescheduled for next week." Tyler went over to the fridge, pulling it open and bending to peer inside. Looking at him in profile, I felt the steel in my resolve melting. I wanted to be mad, indignant. But seeing the sculpted angles of his chest and back, the way his swim trunks cinched his trim waist, interrupting that darkly exciting treasure trail of hair from his navel down to his crotch, I found myself unable to keep up my directive.

Remember Alisha-butterface-McKenna.

"You could have stayed in bed, then," I said as Tyler came back with two hard-boiled eggs—we kept them cooked and peeled in the fridge for a handy, protein-rich, healthy snack—and the carton of goat's milk. He liked it in his coffee, instead of creamer.

"Nah." He made a face, talking through a mouthful of egg. He'd shoved the whole thing in his mouth. "No fun without you."

"So... when did you talk to Alisha McKenna?" I decided to just bring it up, no fuss or drama, pushing the paper across the table, past the coffee pot and carton of milk.

Tyler swallowed, looking down at the headline, and then back up at me. I saw something flicker in his eyes, then he sighed.

"Fuck."

"Yeah," I agreed, sitting back and cinching the tie on my cream silk robe a little tighter before crossing my arms over my chest—which, I had to admit, was nowhere near as impressive as Alisha McKenna's. "My phone's been ringing off the hook. I haven't answered it—I didn't know what to say."

"Fuck," he said again, picking up the paper, his gaze scanning down as he read the article. "I told her not to say anything."

"Did you?" I raised my eyebrows, feeling something tighten in my chest. "What else did you tell her not to say?"

Tyler looked up at me, cocking his head when he saw my expression, and then he grinned.

"Baby, you jealous?"

"Should I be?" I lifted an eyebrow at him, trying to make light of it.

"Never." His gaze softened and he slid out of his seat and switched sides, snugging up next to me. His trunks were still wet, and cold seeped into the side of my robe, but I didn't care when he put his arm around me and nuzzled my ear. "There's no one but you, baby."

"So you told her you were leaving the band?" I couldn't quite let it go, even with his reassuring presence next to me.

"It wasn't like that…" he said. "She was on the set last week, when I had that meeting with Arnie? She stopped me for just a few minutes. You know how she is…"

"Oh, I know." My snarky tone elicited a chuckle from him.

"I just… I didn't really say I was leaving the band. I was tired—and I said it was getting to be too much. The show, recording, and next summer, we'll be going back on tour. How in the hell am I supposed to do it all…?"

"I know. It's a lot." This is just what we'd been talking about, round and round. I swallowed down the fact that he'd said all of this to Alisha McKenna. What I really wanted was to get to the center of the issue. "So… now what?"

"Fuck," he said again, pulling me closer, tucking my head under his chin where it fit perfectly. "Rob. The band is gonna freak."

"Arnie," I reminded him and he groaned.

Their agent, Arnie, was going to take it the hardest. Even though Arnie been the one to get Tyler the audition for *Album* in the first place—and he was the only other person Tyler had told about his condition—Arnie'd gone ostrich about the fact that Tyler's time in the band was physically limited. He definitely wouldn't be happy about this leaking to the press.

"I guess it's time to tell them," Tyler said softly.

My heart got caught in my throat. I lifted my head to look at him, blinking in surprise. I'd suspected that Alisha-*just-gimme-a-minute-of-your-time*-McKenna had stretched the truth—at least, once

I stopped seeing green and being jealous and I started thinking more rationally, that's what I thought—but hearing Tyler say it out loud, making it real, really stunned me.

"For real?" I swallowed, searching his face.

He was tired—those dark circles under his eyes they covered up in make-up were the result of five a.m. shoots and late-night recording sessions. Never mind the nights he spent tossing and turning beside me in bed. He'd been pulled taut, like a guitar string tuned too tight, ready to snap. Something had to give.

"I guess so... yeah." He squeezed me against him, tossing the paper on the table.

"You guess so?" I raised my eyebrows, putting my arms around his neck. "Ty, you need to be sure. This isn't something to guess about."

"I don't know, maybe I knew what I was doing..." His gazed shifted away from mine, then back again. "When I said that—I was in a hurry, I was tired, it was off the cuff, but... maybe some part of me knew, if it came out in the press, then I'd have to..."

"To?" I prompted when his voice trailed off.

"To face it." He made a face, slightly pained. "To decide. It's time, Katie. I just... I can't do it anymore."

"Trouble?"

He nodded.

"So it's over."

We both heard the front door slam.

"Tyler!" Rob. His voice shook the whole house. There weren't many people who had the security code to the gate at the front of the property.

- 11 -

"You forgot to set the alarm again when you came in last night, didn't you?" I rolled my eyes as Tyler slid off the bench seat, but he didn't get far, because Rob was already stomping down the hallway toward the kitchen.

"Goddamnit, Tyler, where are you?"

"Right here, bruh." Tyler leaned opened the fridge, reaching in as Rob burst into the kitchen, his face a storm cloud.

"What the fuck?" Rob frowned at his brother as Tyler took an organic yogurt out of the fridge, closing the door. "You guys don't answer your phones anymore?"

"I was out for a swim." Tyler shrugged as he pulled the lid off his yogurt, finding a spoon in the dishwasher. His nonchalance in the face of his brother's anger only served to make Rob even madder. I knew that look.

"Did you see the article?" Rob's gaze dropped from me to the kitchen table, where the paper was still open, screaming the headline. "Did you talk to her? Is it true?"

"Yeah." Tyler nodded, spooning yogurt into his mouth as he leaned back against the kitchen counter. I looked between the two of them, holding my breath. I had a feeling this wasn't going to end well.

"Yeah?" Rob repeated, looking stunned. "Yeah to which part?"

"All of it," Tyler replied calmly, licking the back of his spoon.

I waited for Rob's explosion. He didn't get mad often, but when he did, it was usually spectacular— and often involved breaking things. Fortunately,

- 12 -

there wasn't much out in the kitchen for him to break, unless he grabbed one of the cast iron pans off the stove and started beating on the marble floor.

It probably would have happened, if Sabrina hadn't appeared, breathless, in the doorway, with a baby on her hip and a barely-walking toddler holding her hand.

"Rob," she said, a warning in her voice. She glanced over at me, giving me an apologetic smile. "Hey guys, sorry to bust in like this. We couldn't get you on the phone, and we were a little worried..."

I raised my eyebrows at that—we all knew it was a lie. They were worried, all right, but not about our personal well-being. They were worried that what they'd read in *Variety* was the truth. Tyler was leaving Trouble.

The truth hadn't fully sunk in yet, even for me.

Trouble without Tyler was like peanut butter without jelly. Impossible.

"It's true." Rob turned to his wife as Sabrina came fully into the kitchen. "It's all fucking true."

"Rob," Sabrina spoke in that warning tone again, glancing at the kids. Their littlest one wasn't old enough to repeat it, but the toddler was.

Lucy saw me and brightened, letting go of her mother's hand and running toward the kitchen table, squealing, "Aunt Katie!" I caught her before she could run into it, tickling her and making her giggle. Tyler smiled, finishing the last of his yogurt and tossing the spoon in the sink.

"I can't believe you didn't tell me." Rob looked at his brother, not angry anymore, and I could sympathize with the hurt, betrayed look in his eyes.

Then he asked the million-dollar question, the one I knew Tyler wouldn't answer. "Why?"

"It's really true?" Sabrina carried the baby over—Henry was a big-eyed, dark-haired butterball—sliding onto the bench seat across from me at the kitchen table, and she asked her question in my direction. "Did you know?"

"I... no." I shook my head, meeting Tyler's eyes. "Not really. Not... officially."

Sabrina gave me a look, like she wasn't sure she quite believed me.

"Why?" Rob asked again, watching Tyler throw his yogurt container away and join me at the kitchen table. Little Lucy was happy to see him and put her chubby arms around his neck, giving him one of those sloppy, open-mouthed kisses toddlers give.

"What are you so pissed about?" Tyler asked, laughing and wiping saliva off his cheek. I had to smile. Thank goodness for babies—it was keeping everyone's temper from edging into the red. "Maybe the label will let Sabrina join the band now."

Rob crossed his arms, leaning against the kitchen island, glaring at the cozy scene we made. Clearly he wasn't ready to concede and join us at the table.

"Oh come on, Ty," Sabrina protested. "You know we never wanted you out. It wasn't about that. It's never been about that."

"Oh I know." Tyler pushed the coffee pot out of Lucy's reach. "But if the label's faced with no Trouble at all, or Trouble-plus-Sabrina, they're going to choose door number two."

"Maybe." Rob scowled, but he uncrossed his arms. "But we didn't want it this way. Besides, Sabrina's doing just fine on her own."

Sabrina had recorded her own album, which had gone platinum, and she'd opened for Trouble last year on tour. It was a good compromise, and it had worked really well. Except that Sabrina had been just-barely pregnant with Henry at the time, so she was extra-tired, and had morning sickness. They'd brought Lucy on tour, along with a nanny who seemed more interested in Rob than she had been in taking care of the baby. They'd fired her halfway through the tour, and I ended up nanny-ing for the rest, which is why Lucy loved me so much now.

"Ty..." Sabrina shifted the baby on her hip, keeping Henry's chubby hand from reaching for a coffee mug. She looked both sad and concerned. "What is it? Are you unhappy?"

"No." Tyler shook his head, distracted by Lucy's attempts to reach the coffee pot he'd placed out of her reach. "No, really. It's not that."

"So what is it?" Rob came over to slide in next to Sabrina at the table. His son smiled and reached for him, and Rob took Henry from Sabrina. "What the hell is it, man? What did we do?"

"It's not you." Tyler sighed and I put my hand on his arm, a silent gesture of support. I had no idea what he was going to tell them was he about to spill everything? I just wanted him to know, whatever he decided, I was there. I would always be there.

He glanced at me over Lucy's dark head—she looked exactly like Sabrina—giving me the ghost of a smile before he looked across the table to face his brother.

"It's not you, it's me?" Rob scoffed. "Is that where you're going with this?"

"No." Tyler shook his still-wet head. "It's… well, yeah. I guess it is me. I just can't do it all."

"That goddamned series." Rob handed the baby back over to Sabrina, and I could tell he was ready to go off again, whether the kids were in the room or not. "It's been a huge distraction from day one. I don't even know why Arnie got it for you. What the fuck was he thinking?"

"He got it for me because I asked him to," Tyler said softly.

"If you're going to quit something, then quit *that*," Rob snapped.

"Rob," Sabrina said for the third time, although the warning in her tone was sharp enough this time that it made Henry start to cry. "Don't."

"Fuck that." Rob slammed his fist on the table, making the coffee pot and mugs jump, but not topple, and Lucy started crying, too. "This isn't happening. I'm not letting this happen."

"You don't have a choice." Tyler let a sniffling Lucy go and she climbed into my lap, sucking her thumb, but it only took her a moment to notice she was closer to the elusive coffee pot. Rob's face grew darker at his brother's words—he didn't like hearing that he didn't have control. "I quit."

"You have a contract," Sabrina reminded him softly.

"I know." Tyler shrugged one shoulder. "They can sue me. I can afford it."

"Jesus." Rob sat back, looking stunned and defeated. "Why? Tyler, why are you doing this?"

"I have to."

"You don't have to," Rob protested. "If you're overworked, we can cut back. We can... do something... but you can't just quit. You can't—"

"I have to." Tyler closed his eyes for a moment, with a little shake of his head, and I knew then, he was going to tell them. I edged closer, still holding Lucy between us.

"You don't—" Rob tried to make the same protest again, but Tyler stopped him with just two words.

"I'm sick."

The silence was like the weight of the world. It stretched forever, until Lucy squealed and put her arms around Tyler's neck to give him another kiss. He accepted it, and her, holding her in his lap. Sabrina's eyes were filling with tears.

"Sick?" Rob could barely get the word out. There was a horror in his eyes I remembered experiencing the first time Tyler told me, too. "Sick how?"

"I'm not dying or anything." Tyler was quick to dispel that, seeing how Sabrina was welling up. "But I've got... I was diagnosed with rheumatoid arthritis. The pain in my hands... I... I can't play anymore. Not like I used to."

"That's why you had the studio musicians in on the album." The realization crossed Rob's face as he sat back, looking even more stunned now than he had when he first walked in. "It wasn't because you were busy with the series. It was because..."

Rob's voice trailed off, like he couldn't even say the words. As if saying the words might make it true. He looked like he wanted to wake up from a living nightmare. I knew that feeling.

"Yeah," Tyler agreed with a grimace. "I'm sorry. I should have told you. I just... I wanted to go as long as I could."

"Tyler, I'm so sorry." Sabrina's tears were falling now, and just looking at her made me want to cry. "Is it... I mean, are you sure? You got a second opinion?"

"A second opinion," Rob repeated, hope flitting across his face. "Good idea. Look, bruh, we can afford the best treatments, the finest doctors. We can—"

"Been there, done that, got the t-shirt," Tyler told them with a sad little smile. "They've got me on the best meds. And changing my diet has helped."

"That's why you stopped the junk food!" Sabrina exclaimed, looking over at me. I just nodded.

"But there's no cure," Tyler said, looking across the table at his brother. "You can't fix this, bruh."

"Fuck." Rob put his head in his hands, elbows on the table.

"Yeah," Tyler agreed.

What more was there to say?

Rob warned Tyler that Arnie wasn't going to take it well—and neither was the label. Or the rest of the band. But there wasn't anything anyone could do about it. Tyler simply couldn't physically do it much longer, and his argument—that he didn't want to let everyone down mid-album or mid-tour—was a sound one. Quitting now would give Trouble time to regroup and decide what direction they wanted to go.

"Call me," Sabrina whispered into my ear when she hugged me goodbye.

I nodded my agreement, handing Lucy over before they went out the door. I'd given Lucy part of a banana to gnaw on, and I had half of it in my hair. She seemed fascinated with the way the light caught in the blonde strands and couldn't keep her sticky hands off it.

"I need a shower," I announced when Tyler closed the front door.

"I need a vacation." He turned and took me in his arms, laughing when I showed him the clumps of banana in my hair.

"That was really brave," I told him, kissing the side of his neck. "I'm so sorry, baby. I know you didn't want to have to do that."

"Let's get the hell out of here." He pulled back to look at me, half-smiling.

"Where to?" I smiled back. It was relief, having the truth out in the open, the last vestige of his secret told.

"Away." His hands moved down to cup my ass. I squealed when he gave it a good squeeze. "Far, far away. Somewhere no one can find us."

"The paparazzi is always watching." I made a face. I understood the inclination, wanting to run away—this news would make the press swarm around us, wherever we went. "Where can we go?"

"How about your mom's?" he suggested after a moment, and I laughed until I almost choked. Then I looked at his face and saw he wasn't kidding.

"You're not kidding?"

"No one would think to look there." He grinned. "Think she'd have us?"

"You really want to sleep on a fold-out couch and eat oatmeal out of a box?" I asked, hoping to dissuade him.

"You're so spoiled." He laughed. "Come on— we'll dodge the paparazzi and fly commercial."

"First-class?" I asked hopefully and he laughed again.

"Come on, spoiled brat, let's go on an adventure."

I wasn't keen on spending time at home with my mother, but I couldn't resist the mischievous look in Tyler's eyes.

I never could say no to him.

Chapter Two

"We should pitch a tent," Tyler said over his shoulder. He stood looking out the second-story window at my mother's property. It was, admittedly, kind of pretty. She had ten acres, most of it wooded, and there was a little pond out back.

"There are bugs outside," I reminded him sleepily, patting his pillow. "Come back to bed."

"I saw a deer." He was sipping coffee, which meant he'd already been down to visit the kitchen. I wondered if my mother was awake. It was a Saturday, so she didn't have to work. "And the raccoons really want to get into the garbage bin. They're like *Ocean's Eleven* out there."

I laughed. "That's why she locks it."

"And there's some sort of crane or something fishing in the pond."

"There are no fish," I told him, pulling his side of the covers back and patting the mattress. My mother had installed a queen size bed in my old room, making it into a guest room, so at least we didn't have to sleep together in a twin or on the pull-out in the living room. "It's too shallow."

"Wonder what he's eating then?" Tyler frowned out the window.

"Frogs." I kicked more of the covers off, exposing my thigh and hip. "Come back to bed."

He glanced back, eyes lighting up when he saw me. "Tempting."

"That's the idea." I held my arms out and he padded toward me in his boxers, putting his coffee on the night stand before slipping back in beside me.

"You are so delicious," he murmured, pulling me close. "And I'm starving."

"Well, we can't have that." I put my arms around his neck and kissed him. His mouth was soft, relaxed, opening under mine, and I delighted in it.

I hadn't realized how tense things had been back home, how much we'd been holding on to all this time. Honestly, when Tyler had suggested coming here, I was horrified—then dubious. Staying with my mother wasn't exactly my idea of a vacation, and I thought for sure it would be a disaster.

But I'd forgotten how charming Tyler could be— and how much my mother liked him, in spite of the fact that he'd gotten her daughter hooked on heroin once upon a time. It seemed she had forgiven and forgotten, and she welcomed us both with open arms. We hadn't seen her since our wedding, although I called her once a month just to check in, and we'd sent her gifts on her birthday and Christmas.

The commercial flight hadn't been bad at all— even though we were both used to a private jet—and the further we got from California, the more we both seemed to be able to breathe easier. Maybe it was the northern Michigan air—we took a little puddle jumper plane into the local airport from Detroit Metro—but it seemed like I could fill my lungs more than ever before.

We'd gone for long walks down the path through the woods every day since we'd arrived, holding hands and not talking. I wanted to ask him what he was thinking—and he was more thoughtful than usual—but he was so happy otherwise. His smile came easier, and so did his laugh. We played card games at night with my mother, or watched TV together, and it seemed so natural, so Midwestern and *normal*. I guess I'd been in California so long, I'd forgotten not everyone lived like we did in Hollywood.

"My mom's home," I whispered, as Tyler kissed his way down my throat. "We'll have to be quiet."

"*You'll* have to be quiet," he reminded me with a chuckle. "Let's see how you do."

Then he covered my nipple with his mouth. I bit my lip to keep from crying out and dug my nails in his shoulder—punishment for teasing me. Tyler hadn't shaved all week and he rubbed his stubble over my skin, leaving a trail of beard-burn down my belly. He dipped his tongue into my navel, a little preview, and I shivered.

"Tyler," I whispered, pushing him lower, lower. I groaned when he went past his implied destination to nuzzle my thighs with his prickly pre-beard. "Oh God, please…"

"Please what?" He parted my thighs with his palms, kissing my inner thigh between his fingers. "Tell me."

"Ty…" I pleaded, my fingers moving through his hair—it was longer than usual, because *Album* was set during the seventies, when guys let it grow. I made a fist in it, pressing my hips up. "I'm begging you…"

"Not yet, you're not." He grinned up at me from between my legs.

"Is that what you want?" I asked. "To make me beg?"

"Say it." He parted me with his fingers, splaying my pussy open, taking in the sight. I could feel his breath, warm against my sex, and shivered. God, I wanted his mouth.

"I want your mouth," I whispered, rocking my hips. "Please, lick me."

"Mmmm, good girl," he praised, and then he dove in.

And I cried out, surely loud enough for my mother to hear, if she was listening or nearby, but by then, I didn't care. I felt Tyler chuckle at my response, but I didn't care about that either, because his skilled tongue was making my hips tilt and my nipples harden and my juices flow down toward the mattress.

"Don't stop," I whispered, both my hands in his hair now, making the same circles with my pelvis that he was making with his tongue. "Oh fuck! Ty!"

"Mmmm!" he managed, but there was no other response, because I was coming all over his face, panting and gasping and quivering all over. I managed to bite back a scream by throwing my forearm arm over my mouth and literally biting down.

God, he made me crazy. He made me a slave to my lust for him. It was shameless, the way he made me beg and wiggle and squirm.

"My turn." Tyler rose up over me, kissing me on the mouth, forcing his tongue in, making me taste myself. I sucked greedily at his tongue, feeling the heat of his erection through his boxers, hard against my thigh.

"Gimme," I gasped when we parted, my hand already snaking under the elastic of his boxers to grasp him in my fist.

"All yours, baby," he assured me, letting me push him to his back on the mattress, lifting his hips as I yanked his boxers down. His cock sprang free, beautifully hard, making my mouth water in anticipation.

"Now it's your turn to be quiet." I gave him an evil grin and he laughed, but that stopped when I slid him into my mouth. I loved watching his face when I sucked him, the way he drew his lower lip between his teeth, the way his brow started to knit the closer he got to coming. He let out a low moan when I took all of him—as much as I possibly could, anyway—deep into my throat.

"Fuck," he whispered, opening his eyes to watch me come up on his length, stopping to trace my tongue around the head. He shuddered when I did that, grabbing a handful of my hair.

"Shhh," I reminded him, licking the frenulum, teasing, back and forth. "Gotta be quiet, remember?"

"Stop talking." He pressed my head down. "Keep sucking."

So I did, no longer teasing. I sucked him—long, hard, cheek-hollowing strokes from tip to base. Tyler managed to keep his groans to a minimum, although the hand in my hair got tighter and tighter as he guided me up and down his length, setting my pace. I loved it when he did that.

"Wait, wait," he gasped, pulling me off. My lips felt swollen and hot from the friction. I looked up at him through half-closed eyes, feeling my pussy throbbing, aching for him. "I want to fuck you."

"This bed makes too much noise," I reminded him hoarsely, although my clit quivered just thinking about having him inside of me. We'd tried fucking the first night we were here, but the mattress squeaked like there was a mouse trapped between it, so we'd resigned ourselves to quieter versions of sex for the week, at least when my mother was home.

"I can fix that." Tyler got up, taking me with him.

My mother had bought all new furniture for the "guest bedroom," as it was now called—funny, my older brother's room had been left exactly the same, but my room had become the "guest bedroom"—and that set included a bed, two night stands, and a long dresser with a mirror attached.

"What are you doing?" I whispered, glancing at the closed door as Tyler put his arms around me, edging me backwards.

"Fucking you," he growled, grabbing my ass in both hands and lifting me until I was sitting on the dresser. It was the perfect height.

"Ty!" I hissed his name, my arms going instinctively around his neck, clinging. "Wait."

"No." His cock rode the seam of my slit, up and down. "Put your legs over my shoulders."

"Put my… what?"

Tyler shifted his weight, sliding his arms under my knees, forcing my feet up over his shoulders, folding me practically in half.

"Oh God, Ty," I panted, but then he was inside me, filling me.

I moaned—not softly either—as he started to fuck me, deep and hard. The dresser rocked a little, but the mirror had been anchored to the wall, so there was no banging of a headboard, no squeaking of the bedsprings.

"Harder," I whispered, meeting his eyes, so dark with lust it made me feel faint. "Fuck me, Ty. Fuck me harder."

He did, driving deeper, bottoming out with each thrust. My clit ached and I reached down with one hand—keeping the other looped around his neck for balance—rubbing furiously. He moaned when I did that, hips pistoning into me like a machine.

"Gonna come," he panted, voice hoarse. "Oh baby, I can't... I can't—"

"Yessss!" I hissed, my pussy already starting to spasm. I was so wet, I was sure my juices were dripping down the front of my mother's new cherry wood dresser, and we were about to christen it even further.

"Come for me," he groaned, fucking me so hard he forced my breath out in short, hot pants. "Come for me, now!"

I did, grinding back against him, my heels digging into his shoulders, feeling his cock pulsing deep inside of me. I felt every hot pulse of his orgasm, and I was glad that he captured my mouth with his, drowning both our moans of pleasure in a hard, desperate, greedy kiss. We shuddered and clung to each other.

Tyler grabbed my hips, letting my legs down so I could wrap them around his waist, and he carried me like that back to the bed. He didn't slide out of me, though. He stayed in, putting me on the mattress, shoving me down with his hips as he moved on top of me.

"I love you, Katie," he whispered, still moving, his cock only half-hard. "God, I love you."

His words made me melt, brought instant tears to my eyes. I couldn't imagine loving a man more than I loved this one. I felt sorry for other women, who didn't have Tyler. And God knows, there were plenty who wanted him. But I was the one he wanted. I was the one he'd chosen.

"I love you, too," I whispered back, welcoming the weight of him, wanting it all. I felt completely taken by him this way, when he curled his body around me and let himself rut deep, as if he could push all of himself inside of me and stay there.

His breath grew ragged in my ear, but his movements never increased. It was a slow, easy, delicious sort of fuck, perfectly timed and controlled. The bed springs didn't make any noise at all, but I did, crying out when he made me come yet again, before he came again, too, whispering my name like the sweetest song in my ear.

We laid there for a while, just like that, connected, feeling whole and content. We probably would have fallen back asleep eventually, but then my mother knocked on the door.

"Katie?"

"Just a minute, Mom!" I called, trying find the covers—but we were on them.

"Just wondered if you two wanted to go out for breakfast?"

I met Tyler's eyes and shrugged, telling him silently that it was up to him.

"Sure!" Tyler agreed. "Give us a minute to get ready."

We hadn't gone anywhere out in public since we got here—I think both of us had agreed, without talking about it, that holing up would keep the rest of the world away. There was no paparazzi up here— but if we went out in public, someone could recognize Tyler—even in the Midwest, everyone knew Trouble—and before long, everyone would know where we were.

"When she says breakfast, she means the local *Greasy Spoon*," I said as he climbed off me and reached for his boxers.

"Nothing wrong with that," he told me, yanking on his jeans. "I love *Diners, Drive-Ins and Dives*. Everyone needs a little greasy spoon in their lives."

"No, I mean literally—the local diner is called *The Greasy Spoon*."

He stopped in mid-button. "You're kidding."

"Serious as a heart attack." I grinned back at him. "Which is what you'll have if you eat there."

"You know me. I love to live dangerously." He laughed. "Besides, it will make your mom happy."

"Okay, let's go eat junk food." I relented. "But not too much. I need these talented hands functional, mister."

"Yes, ma'am."

* * * *

"Rob and Sabrina's babies are getting so big," my mother remarked over bacon and eggs. "They sent me a Christmas card. Beautiful family."

"Yes, ma'am," Tyler agreed, sopping up his eggs with toast. I was sure the eggs weren't organic, and I didn't even want to think about what was in the toast—and the fructose-filled jelly he'd slathered on it—but we were splurging.

"Tyler, you can call me 'Mom'," she admonished, for like the millionth time that weekend.

"Yes, ma'am," he agreed, then realized what he'd said and quickly corrected himself. "Uhhh—Mom."

"Better." She laughed. "So... when are you two going to have one?"

I knew this subject was going to come up eventually. I was surprised she'd waited this long. I caught Tyler's eye and he shrugged.

"Twelfth of never." I gave her a dark look over the rim of my coffee cup.

"Well, that's probably best," she said, stirring sugar into her coffee. Oh, the snark. *Gee, thanks, Mom,* I thought but didn't say. Then she looked up and saw the expression on my face. "I just mean, you know, you have so much going on, between Trouble's tour and the series."

Right. What I saw on her face was, "You can barely take care of yourself, let alone a child."

But she wouldn't say that, at least, not in front of Tyler. She'd probably say it later, just to me. She couldn't hold it back forever—I knew that much. She'd let it slip, one way or another. Luckily, the waitress came over and interrupted the track this conversation was on.

"If I can get you anything else..." The waitress put the bill down on the table. "Just let me know..."

"Thanks." My mother smiled up at her.

The waitress turned to go, but then she stopped, turning back to look at Tyler.

"I'm sorry, but... are you..." The waitress glanced across the restaurant, then looked back at Tyler. I knew what was coming. "It's just... the girls over there at that table were wondering... aren't you Tyler Cook?"

My stomach sank when I looked over at the table full of teens, whispering behind their hands and giggling. I met Tyler's eyes and saw that little edge was back, a slight stiffness in his shoulders, and cursed my mother's idea to go to breakfast.

"What would Tyler Cook be doing here?" I asked the waitress, holding out my half-full coffee mug. "Think you can get me some more coffee? This is cold."

"Sure." The waitress—her name tag said Elaine—gave me a nod, a look of confusion on her face.

She knew it was Tyler—probably knew who I was, too. Our wedding had been a day of mourning among Trouble and Tyler Cook fans everywhere. But it was hard to contradict someone politely when they said they weren't who you thought they were. At least, outside of Hollywood. In Hollywood, you couldn't pretend, like I was now. The spotlights—and the odds—were too good there.

"It's not getting any warmer," I prompted, and Elaine flushed and turned toward the kitchen. The girls looked up at her expectantly as she approached the table, shaking her head, and there was a little outburst of disbelief and more glances our way as she delivered her news.

"You didn't have to be rude, Katie," my mother said, keeping her voice low. "I have to live here. Besides, everyone knows already."

"I'm sure they do." I sighed, seeing the way Tyler's spine straightened. Waiting for fans to approach was like putting on armor. "I was just buying us a little time. Do you want to go?"

I was talking to Tyler, not my mother.

"It's okay." He was watching the table out of the corner of his eye, I could tell. So was I. The girls were whispering and talking and gathering up their courage. It wouldn't take them long before they decided, and then one of them would approach, since their send-the-waitress plan had failed.

"We just wanted to keep a low profile, remember?" I reminded my mother, who started to protest. "You don't want a million people swarming the house, do you?"

"There aren't anywhere near a million people in these parts, Katie."

"It's just an expression." I rolled my eyes.

And then they were coming over. Not one of them, but all four of them.

"Would you sign my napkin?" The tall one, darkly pretty for a Midwestern girl, clearly the confident ringleader, held out a pen and a clean napkin to Tyler.

- 32 -

"Sure." He didn't deny her—he never did. I was the one who tried to protect him, when I could, from situations like this. The first couple times you had your meal interrupted by a fan weren't awful, but eventually, it got exhausting. Still, Tyler was always sweet to fans. Too sweet, in my not-so-humble opinion, as I watched him lean over and smile so each girl could take a selfie with him.

"Thank you so much. You're the best. You're bae!" the tall, confident girl gushed, and I gritted my teeth when she quickly stole a kiss from Tyler—on the lips, no less—before running off to join her girlfriends, who were already back, giggling around their table.

"Bae?" My mother blinked in surprise, clearly taken aback by the whole scene. "What in the world?"

"It's a think the kids say," Tyler told her, smiling over at me. It hadn't been that long ago that I was one of those "kids," going to Trouble concerts and screaming myself hoarse. Granted, "bae" wasn't an expression back then—we called good-looking guys "hotties"—but the sentiment and the silliness was the same.

"It means 'before anyone else'," I told her. "At least, that's how it started. The kids call their boyfriends and girlfriends 'bae'."

My mother wrinkled her nose. "But they don't even know you."

"They think they do." Tyler shrugged.

"Girls say it when they see a cute guy," I explained. "*He's so bae.* Or *he's my bae*—even if he's some celebrity she's never met."

"I think we'd better go." My mother nodded toward the waitress, who was finally coming back to fill my coffee cup. She didn't look happy.

"Oh, she knew I was lying." I sighed, pushing the chair back from the table. "Ty will make her happy. Come on, Mom, let's go pay."

Of course, Tyler was sweet to the waitress, too, and signed an autograph for her on her pad—and let her take a selfie. I gritted my teeth while I paid the bill and my mother said how kind Tyler was to his fans, and it wasn't until we were out of the restaurant, headed to the car, that I finally said something.

"Don't you get it?" I snapped, as she unlocked the car with her key fob. "Those selfies they took in there? Guaranteed they've already been posted to those girls' Facebook pages or put up on Instagram. We've got twenty-four hours, maybe forty-eight, before the press shows up."

"Here?" She laughed, but then she saw the serious look on my face. "Surely they wouldn't come up here...?"

"Well, it was fun while it lasted, eh?" Tyler said, jogging up to join us. "Thanks for the hospitality, Mom. I really loved staying at your place."

"You don't have to go?" She looked between the two of us, then back at the restaurant, where we could see the girls around the table, all of them with their phones in their hands. "Just because of that?"

My phone buzzed in my pocket and I sighed. *Already?*

"Who is it?" Tyler asked as I pulled it out to check.

We'd told Rob and Sabrina where we were going, and why—they both assured us they'd handle the fallout and the press for a week or two. Rob even said he'd handle Arnie and the label. Maybe we'd taken advantage of their shock, running away while the devastation was still fresh, but I didn't really care.

I looked at my phone, expecting to see Sabrina's number, but it wasn't. It was a desperate text.

I need help. I'm in California. Can I come see you?

"Who is it?" Tyler peered over my shoulder.

"It's Jay." I blinked back at him. "She's in California. Looking for us."

"Who's Jay?" my mother asked.

"It's a long story." One I wasn't going to tell her, if I could help it. "We should go home."

Tyler sighed. "I guess our vacation's over."

Chapter Three

We couldn't fly commercial home. Couldn't even take the little puddle jumper from the local airport back to Detroit Metro. That's how fast it happened. We managed to get back to my mom's place and pack our stuff—all the while, my mother dismissed our fast-acting as paranoia—before the first car appeared in the driveway.

"I guess I should get a gate," my mother muttered, peering out the window. "That's Ed from our little local paper—does he really think he's going to get some sort of scoop?"

"He's just holding down the fort and waiting for reinforcements," I told her. "Hopefully, we'll be long gone by the time that happens."

"Is this really want your life is like, all the time?" my mother asked, incredulous.

"This is nothing," Tyler told her with a laugh. "You should see us going to Starbucks on a Wednesday."

Her eyes got bigger when another car showed up. "Who could possibly care that much about what you do with your life?"

"The whole damned world."

While Tyler dealt with my mother, who stood by the window like our own internal reporter, telling us what the reporters outside were up to—local channel WKDB news had shown up—I texted with Jay.

When it rained, it poured.

I ran away.

I knew it was only a matter of time before she pulled something like this. Her home life had been deteriorating for years, but it was far worse now than when I'd met her on my first tour with Tyler and Trouble. She'd been just thirteen then, breathtakingly beautiful and naïve, hanging out with girls who were older than her and able to get into a lot more trouble than she would have been capable of on her own.

Including flirting their way onto Trouble's tour bus, and getting their hands on an 8-ball of heroin. Ah, youth. It had been my first tour with Trouble, and while I was nowhere near as naïve, three underage girls with hard drugs, all three of them ready to spread their legs for payment, had shocked me. I'd given all three of them a good talking-to—reminding myself eerily of my own mother—and then I'd put them on a bus and sent them back to their hometown in the middle of the country.

Except Jess. She was the littlest one—actually just twelve, although she'd lied and told me she was thirteen—and so in love with Rob Burns of Trouble that she was willing to run away from home to meet him. Like any star-struck kid, she was certain that just showing up on Rob's doorstep would be enough. One look at her, and true love would kick in—he'd whisk her away with him to his castle in the sky. Or in the Hollywood hills. Same difference.

Problem was, Jess had no idea that Rob Burns, recently almost-divorced, was madly in love with my best friend, Sabrina. Who also just happened to be pregnant with his love-child. Because while Jess's fantasy hadn't happened to twelve-year-old Jess—it had happened for my twenty-something, elementary school teacher friend, Sabrina.

Sabrina had won the rock star lottery, while Jess was being sent home to parents who loved her, but clearly weren't paying enough attention to their wayward daughter. And they had their own problems, I would soon find out. Dad was an alcoholic. Mom was oblivious, rather neglectful, and seemed to be the type of woman who picked the worst sorts of guys. The kind of guys who struggled to keep a job, the kind of guys who liked to hit their women—and their teenaged daughters—when they were drunk. Which was almost all the time.

Tyler knew I was talking to Jess—her friends called her Jay, and that's what I called her, now, too—and thought it was sweet. A few times, I'd been on the verge of asking him if we could just adopt the poor girl—and Tyler had headed that off on each occasion with, "Katie, we can't keep her. This isn't a stray puppy." I knew he was right.

Besides, every time, something had changed, the situation diffused, and Jay had calmed down enough to go back to school and resume her tumultuous life as a teenage girl. She wasn't the first, and by no means the last, girl who would deal with a horrible home life she longed to escape from. But she was my girl—our girl. I did what I could, from a few thousand miles away, and over the past few years, a sort of bond had developed.

Then, her father had left. At first, I thought it was the best thing that could have happened to Jay and her mother. With her alcoholic father out of the picture, I imagined a single mom and her daughter making their way in the world, sort of an idealized *Gilmore Girls*, without the rich parents. Jay's mother came from solid, middle-class roots, including a typical broken home and parents who lived on opposite ends of the country. Just like me, really.

What I hadn't counted on was Jay's mother, and the hole she felt she needed to fill once the man of the house wasn't living in it anymore. Jay started complaining about her "new daddy" almost right away. He was big, he had a face tattoo like a Celtic half-moon on the side of his face, he rode a motorcycle, and like Jay's father before him, he had a love affair with alcohol. Jay didn't like him, and not only because he had stepped into her father's shoes. She didn't like the way he looked at her when her mother wasn't around—and even though I wasn't there, I didn't like it either.

She never said he did anything to her—maybe she knew, I would have called the cops in a heartbeat. But he was always this looming presence in her life. I found myself talking with Tyler about her more and more, as time went on—I think I was getting him ready for this moment, sort of priming the pump, wearing him down with the devastation of her life. Because I knew this was going to happen, eventually.

Once a runaway, always a runaway.

Where are you?

She answered me with one word—*California*—and I couldn't help but shake my head at the irony. We'd roughly changed places. She'd run to California for help, and here we were, stuck in the Midwest with the press camped outside our door.

So while Tyler called Rob, and Rob figured out how to get us home, with the help of Celeste—his personal assistant and the woman who singlehandedly ran the details of all our lives, when necessary—I dealt with the Jay situation.

She'd hitchhiked her way across country. She was dirty, hungry, broke, and standing on the corner of Hollywood and Vine. I told her to walk down to Capitol Records and wait. Someone would be there to pick her up.

Then, I called Sabrina. We'd been best friends since we were Jay's age, and we'd been inseparable ever since. Our lives had moved forward on this strangely parallel track, like some sort of mirrored image of light and dark.

Sabrina was the good girl—who didn't come from a broken family, who finished school and got a good job, who was sensible and responsible and smart. And I was her dark foil—the bad girl, the one who got herself in trouble more often than not, and dragged Sabrina with me.

Somehow, we'd both ended up with a fairy tale, married to rock star brothers—but our journeys couldn't have been more different. Hers involved babies and marriage and her own career as a singer. Mine involved jumping on a bus to go on tour with the band, a dizzying spiral into drug addiction, from pain-killers to heroin, and a long road of relapse and recovery until it ended with me married to Tyler, the two of us battered and bruised, but so much in love it hurt.

Funny, I wouldn't trade places with Sabrina, not for all the money in the world. Not that either of us needed money—not anymore.

I was still talking to Sabrina, giving her the details about Jay—it was something I'd never shared with my best friend before, so it was all news to her—telling her where to pick her up, when Tyler told me our car had arrived.

"Is she... I mean, is she dangerous?" Sabrina asked me, sounding doubtful.

"She's just fifteen-years-old," I told her, rolling my eyes and nodding to Tyler, holding up one finger in a *wait-a-second* gesture. "How dangerous could she be?"

"I just mean... you know, is she going to steal us blind?" Sabrina sounded reluctant to even say it, but sensible as she was, she couldn't help herself. "Should I put her up in a hotel somewhere instead?"

"No." I scoffed. "She just needs a safe place to stay. Keep her with you until we get home. Then I'll take her off your hands, I promise."

"Okay..." Sabrina still sounded reluctant, but because it was me, I knew she would do what I asked. "Come straight here."

"We will," I promised.

"There will be press at the airport. It's already all over the internet," she told me. "Everyone knows where you are."

"We won't be here long. Car's here now," I said. "I'll see you when we get home. Thanks for this, Sabrina."

"Anything for you, Katie. See you soon."

In spite of the fact that we were on a private jet this time, the flight home was nowhere near as fun or adventurous as the commercial flight we'd taken from California to Michigan. Tyler and I sat alone in the giant cabin, side by side, holding hands but lost in our own thoughts.

I knew he was thinking about what waited for us at home—a barrage of questions from hundreds of paparazzi, and a bevy of screaming, crying teenaged girls desperate to hear that it wasn't true, rock god Tyler Cook couldn't be leaving their favorite band.

It was time to turn rumor into fact. He was going to have to disappoint them all.

I was worried about teen girls, too—one in particular. Sabrina texted me just as we were boarding the plane that Jay was safe and sound at their place, already having fun playing with the babies. That was a relief, at least.

Now I just had to convince Tyler that we needed to keep this particular stray puppy—at least for a little while.

"Katie..." He sighed when I told him my plan. "This is the worst timing ever. Can you imagine the spin on this when the press gets hold of it?"

"No one else needs to know," I assured him.

He shook his head. "We might be able to fly under the radar sometimes, but the spotlight is going to be on us for the next couple weeks at least—we won't be able to take a piss without some reporter following us."

"Someone will do something stupid and the spotlight will shift again," I told him. "We've been through this before."

"In the meantime, you want a fifteen-year-old runaway to move in with us?"

I sighed. "She doesn't have anywhere else to go."

"She could go home."

"No." I shook my head vehemently. "She can't."

"Listen to me." He turned my face toward him. "For a minute. Just try to look at this rationally."

"Rationally?" I cried, knowing I was going to have to tell him something to move him in the right direction. "There's nothing rational about a fifteen-year-old girl being abused by her stepfather. We can't send her back there, Tyler. We can't."

He pursed his lips, thinking. "Okay, I agree with you."

I relaxed a little.

"But we can't keep her, either," he said, and I tensed again. "We have plenty of resources at our disposal. We can get her help. Good, professional help—that doesn't involve her squatting in our living room."

"Tyler, please..." I begged, wrapping my arms around his neck and snuggling close. "She's counting on us. On me."

"I'm not saying no." He sighed, and I felt his body relenting, at least a little. "I'm just saying—let's think about this."

"I have thought about it," I assured him. "If we call the authorities, she'll never speak to me again. And you know, if we do, they'll just send her back."

"They won't put her back there if it's a dangerous environment."

"Oh come on. You know how broken the system is." I rolled my eyes. "And even if they don't send

- 43 -

her home—you grew up in it, Ty. You know what it's like, being a foster kid. Do you want to subject her to that?"

He looked thoughtful. "No."

"So does that mean... can we keep her?"

"Maybe." He sighed again, then laughed when I kissed his cheek over and over in thanks. "Look, let's just take this one step at a time, okay?"

"Okay," I agreed, happy that the answer was 'yes, for now,' instead of an emphatic 'no'. I could live with that, and we could take it one step at a time.

The next step involved getting off the plane and into a car without the press tracking us down. Thanks to Celeste, it turned out to be a breeze. Jesse—Rob's driver—was waiting for us in a Rolls-Royce on the tarmac when we came off the plane.

I hugged him and kissed his cheek, relieved to see someone familiar, and equally relieved to be home. In spite of the fact that I'd lived in Michigan my whole life, I hadn't realized how much I thought of California as "home" until my feet were on the pavement and I could see palm trees in the distance.

Jesse loaded our bags into the back and we got into the car, finding Celeste sitting up front in the passenger seat.

"So what's the damage?" Tyler asked her after she and I exchanged a one-armed over-the-seat hug along with basic pleasantries.

"Not as bad as it could be," Celeste assured him as Jesse got into the driver's side. He leaned over to kiss her and I smiled. Sometimes it still didn't compute—Jesse and Celeste. They were so opposite.

She was straight-laced, buttoned-up, perfectly poised and in control. He was this big, blonde surfer-type dude who wore board shorts and flip-flops—when he wasn't driving, anyway. And even then, Rob didn't make him dress up in a monkey suit, unless he was taking us somewhere formal or meeting someone new.

Still, they were happy together—who could argue with love? Certainly not me. Cupid drew his bow, and we were all at the mercy of his strange aim. Or we could blame the oxytocin hormones. Either way, love was oddly inexplicable, how and where it struck, like a tornado that missed one house but destroyed the one next door.

"What's that mean, exactly?" Tyler asked, and Celeste started filling him in on who had reported what and when, how they were working to spin his decision to leave Trouble, and reassuring him that no one knew the real reason. That last was important to him, I knew—he didn't want anyone to know his diagnosis, especially the producers of *Album*. He was afraid they'd get spooked and believe it would affect his performance.

I half-listened while I texted with Jay.

Katie, these babies are so cute!

I know-how are you doing?

This house is amazing! Huge! I've never been in a house this big!

I know but how are you doing?

Sabrina's a doll. Rob is so nice. Thank you for having them come get me. I can't thank you enough.

Jay-HOW ARE YOU?

Better. Really. I wish I'd run away a long time ago.

Okay then. Denial—not just a river in Egypt.

Not that I didn't understand and sympathize with her reaction. Stepping into Trouble's world was like entering a whole new plane of existence. Houses behind gates, drivers, cooks, housekeepers, giant swimming pools. For a small-town Midwestern girl, it was like an episode of *The Beverly Hillbillies*, except Jay wasn't quite as naïve as Elly May Clampett.

Hang in there--we're on the ground and coming to get you.

Jay texted back—*Thanks.*

"Hey, Jesse, can we go to Rob and Sabrina's first?" I asked, slipping my phone back into my purse.

"That's the plan," Celeste told me, flipping down the visor mirror and smoothing her pulled-back, dark hair. It was always like that, up in a perfectly-coiffed bun.

"You look beautiful, as always." Jesse smiled over at her, a light in his eyes, and I caught a glimpse of what he saw in her—he was the only one who knew what this put-together woman looked like with her hair down. The only one she trusted enough to let it down with. That made me smile, too.

"Why are we going to Rob and Sabrina's?" Tyler frowned, sitting back in his seat and putting a casual arm around my shoulder. I snuggled closer to him.

"So we can pick up Jay," I reminded him.

"Family meeting," Celeste said, at the exact same time. Our eyes met in the visor mirror before she flipped it up. "Daisy's making brunch."

"Well, at least we get some good food," I said when Tyler groaned and rolled his eyes.

"What's there to talk about?" Tyler protested. "It's done. I'm out. My decision's made."

"Come on, Ty." Celeste turned to look at him over the seat. "You don't get out of it that easy. You got to run away for a week—now it's time to come home and face the music. So to speak."

"More like the firing squad," he grumbled.

"No one's out to get you," Celeste told him gently. "They just... they want to hear an explanation. From you, personally."

"So everyone wants to hear me say I'll never play guitar again?" Tyler scowled. "Great. Couldn't we just send out a memo?"

"This is your family, Ty," I reminded him softly. "They're all family—even Arnie and the guys."

He nodded, relenting, but his jaw was still tight. "Fine, but I'm only doing this once."

"Fair enough," Celeste agreed.

"That means I want my mother there." He dropped that bombshell and the car went dead quiet. I could count on one hand the times Tyler's mother had been in the same room with Rob. Tyler and Sarah had come to forgive her, but Rob? He simply couldn't, it seemed.

"Oh... Ty... uhhhh..." Celeste looked at Jesse, then at me. I shrugged. What did she want me to do about it? "That's not a good idea. Rob..."

"Fuck him," he snapped. I winced. I knew he loved his brother—they were incredibly close—but Tyler couldn't understand Rob holding out like this. Their mother had paid her debt to society—that was Tyler's argument. She'd spent years in jail, and had come out changed. But Rob just couldn't see that. Or forgive everything that had happened when they were kids.

"Call her," Tyler insisted. "Get her there. Or I'm not doing this."

Celeste shook her head, but she got her phone out of her purse. "All right."

"He won't let her through the gates," Jesse said, glancing in the rear view to meet Tyler's blazing eyes.

"Then I won't be going through them, either."

"Ty…" I put my hand in his, squeezing gently as Celeste got Leanne on the phone. Tyler had bought my mother-in-law a home in the hills, nothing big and extravagant, but nice. "This *is* a lot to ask."

"It's been years, Katie," he reminded me. "He's ignored her at every holiday we've had at our house—now he can ignore her in his house. What's the difference?"

"Okay, okay," I soothed.

I felt a little shanghaied by this impromptu 'family meeting', and I imagine Tyler felt the same. We'd been set up. It felt a little like we were walking into the lion's den. Or an intervention. Is that what this was about? I wondered. Were they going to try to talk Ty out of quitting the band?

But Rob and Sabrina knew the truth. They knew Tyler had a very good reason. This wasn't just a bored or disgruntled musician who wanted to do something else with his career. This was something Tyler was going to have to live with for the rest of his life, and it was probably the hardest decision he'd ever make. Except maybe the one he'd made a few years ago when he'd decided not to be junkie anymore.

I squeezed his hand and looked up at him. Ty smiled down at me, leaned in to kiss me, a sweet, brief connection. But I saw the pain in his eyes. I don't know if anyone else would have seen it, besides me—it was pushed way back, as far back as he could possibly get it, but it was still there. He was hurting.

"You don't have to," I whispered, nuzzling my cheek against his shoulder. "We can go home instead. You and me, baby."

Tyler's other arm tightened around my shoulder and he gave a slow, sad shake of his head.

"She's right... I have to face the music eventually. Might as well do it now."

"Fast—like pulling off a Band-Aid."

"Right." He laughed, but it was a bitter sound.

"I promise, I'll kiss it and make it better."

"You make everything better," he breathed, kissing me again.

It was the hardest lesson I think I'd ever had to learn. Some things you just couldn't fix, no matter how much you wanted to.

There was a crowd of paparazzi waiting at the gates outside of Rob and Sabrina's place. But the car windows were tinted and Celeste had us duck way down as we approached, so they couldn't get a picture from the front. Once we were inside, we were safe. At least, it felt that way. Granted, we'd had press—and even the occasional obsessed fan—jump the gates before. But Rob had excellent security.

After Catherine, he'd made the place nearly impenetrable.

Thinking about Catherine gave me shivers as we pulled up to the house. It was right here, just over the foot bridge, that Rob's ex-wife had shot Sabrina. It had been a shoulder wound—nothing fatal, thank God—but Sabrina had lost her pregnancy. Poor little Esther. I could still remember the weight of her in my hand, such a tiny thing, a totally senseless loss.

And my fault. It had been my fault that Catherine was there that day—I was the one that let her through the gates. Granted, I hadn't known it was her, but what did it matter? The results had been the same. I didn't like to think about that time—and the downward spiral the followed, my relapse, my shame. I could never make up for what Sabrina and Rob had lost that day.

"You ready for this?" I asked Tyler, taking a deep breath and readying myself.

I could put on a brave face for him. I knew how much it hurt him, quitting the band, but everyone in there, except maybe Rob and Sabrina, was likely to be furious about his decision. I'm sure they all thought it was selfish on his part—but that couldn't be further from the truth. He was giving up something that meant more to him than almost anything.

"Let's get it over with." He shoved the door open and got out.

I followed, hoping I could pick up the pieces once everyone was done ripping him apart.

Chapter Four

You would have thought we were having a party, instead of making an announcement that would end life as we all knew it. It should have been more like a wake—everyone in black, mourning the loss, talking about the good old days—but it wasn't. The mood was far lighter than I expected, even after Leanne had arrived.

That was probably because Sarah brought her. Tyler and Rob's sister, Sarah, was sort of the mediating one in the family. She was the youngest, and if she stood between her two big, towering brothers, she could stop them fighting with a shake of her finger and just one word. It was a talent neither Sabrina or I had perfected, and I admired her for it.

But Sarah was big on doing her own thing, speaking her mind, and telling the truth when no one else was willing to. She and her long-time roommate-slash-lover, Anne, had gotten married last year, after California made gay marriage legal— again. Anne had worn her combat boots under a black lace dress—and Sarah had worn white. They were both stunning, even Anne with her piercings and tattoos.

Leanne appeared between Sarah and Anne. I saw Rob scowl when he saw his mother, and I saw Sabrina nudge him and say something into his ear. After that he stopped scowling, but he pretty much ignored her existence for the rest of the night.

For my part, I went over and kissed Leanne's scarred, ravaged cheek and welcomed her to the gathering. Tyler did the same, whispering, "Thanks for coming, Mom." You'd never know, the way she beamed up at him, that Tyler was the one who had shot her husband in the head when he wasn't quite a teen yet.

More secrets. So many secrets.

I hugged Sarah and Anne, and we chatted for a moment, catching up. But the whole time, I kept an eye on Jay. She was playing with Lucy and Henry, rolling a ball under the big, grand piano and giggling when they chased after it. She looked like such a kid herself, still, even though she was fifteen now. A stunning beauty, with long, dark hair that flowed like a waterfall to her lower back, it was her eyes that captivated. Big, round violet eyes.

"Who's that?" Leanne asked. She'd noticed me keeping an eye on Jay.

"She's..." Oh crap, how was I going to explain Jay? "My cousin. Here for a visit."

It was the best I could do on short notice. Tyler's eyebrows went up but he didn't contradict me.

"Pretty girl." Leanne smiled as Henry, who was crawling now, fought over the ball with his older sister. I felt bad for Leanne. Rob refused to let her have anything to do with her grandchildren. I knew Sabrina had taken them to visit Leanne a few times, without Rob knowing, but it was a tough situation.

Not that I blamed him, exactly. Leanne hadn't exactly been in the running of any Mother of the Year awards when she was arrested on drug use and possession charges and her three kids had been put

- 53 -

into foster care. My mother was a pain in my ass—but I knew she loved me, and I never really wanted for anything, not like Rob and Tyler and Sarah had. I couldn't blame Rob for being angry—nor could I blame Sarah and Tyler for forgiving her and wanting to reconnect. I mean, the woman was their mother—and you only ever got one of those.

"Who's hungry?" Daisy—Rob and Sabrina's cook—appeared in the doorway carrying a tray full of something appetizery that smelled amazing. "There's lots more in the kitchen—anyone want to help me bring them out?"

Of course, Rob and Tyler went to help, and Sarah and Anne did, too. Sabrina stayed to keep an eye on the babies, but they were too busy playing with Jay to notice. I sat on one of the sofas and patted the seat beside me for Leanne. She joined me, looking more than a little uncomfortable being in Rob and Sabrina's house. I could only remember one other time that she'd been there—right after she'd gotten out of jail.

I waved at the other guys in the band—Tyler called them "the three stooges" when they weren't around. They were sitting three across on another sofa, all of them drinking beer, busy on their phones. Nick was the only one who waved back—he was Trouble's third-cutest band member and bass player. Jon, the tall, lanky, bespectacled keyboardist, didn't look up from his phone. Kenny, the almost-chubby drummer, saw me wave but didn't respond.

I'd always thought it was kind of weird, the way the other three members of Trouble were kind of distant. They were in the band, and they certainly reaped the benefits, but they just didn't participate in the more "family" type things that much—and when they did, they stuck together, just like that, the three of them, thick as thieves.

Maybe it was the blood connection between Rob and Tyler—didn't they say blood was thicker than water? But that didn't explain it completely, because for years, no one knew Rob and Tyler were even brothers. That had been yet another secret they'd kept, up until a few years ago, when everything had sort of come crashing down around our heads.

"Do you have any idea why we're here?" Leanne asked, leaning in so she wouldn't be overheard.

"Tyler's got an announcement to make," I told her, glancing up as Tyler and Rob came in carrying more trays full of food. My stomach growled.

"Are you?" Leanne's hand rested on my forearm and I looked down at it, then up at the bright look in her eyes—well, one eye. The other was glass and didn't see anything—the one on the scarred side of her face. "Oh Katie, are you expecting?"

"No!" I exclaimed, shaking my head. "No, it's not that."

"Oh, okay then." She sighed, sitting back against the sofa and I fought the urge to roll my eyes. Did every mother-type-person want grandkids this bad?

"Someday," I lied. I knew better. Tyler didn't want kids—and I wasn't sure about it myself. Not that I didn't like them. I loved kids, and watching Sabrina with hers made my ovaries vibrate like they were going to just explode, but we'd been through so much, before and after we had gotten married, I just hadn't had enough time to really consider it.

"Is this about the band breaking up then?" Leanne asked and I looked at her and sighed. "I read the article in *Variety* on the plane."

"The plane?"

"Sarah went with me to go through my mother's things." She smiled up at Sarah as she approached with a plate full of appetizers for her mother. Leanne accepted them and my stomach growled again. "We were there for about a week. We just got back."

"Your mother?" I felt like I was repeating everything she said, trying to make sense of it.

"Our grandmother," Sarah explained, perching on the edge of the sofa with her own plate. "She passed, about a month ago. We had to go through her house so we could put it up for sale."

"Oh, I'm sorry, I didn't know." I glanced over at Tyler, who was talking with Rob by the grand piano, where the kids were still playing around the legs. Jay crawled around under there with them, chasing the ball, all of them giggling.

Why hadn't Tyler told me?

"Liver failure. She was an alcoholic. Drank herself to death," Leanne said. "Her drug of choice just happened to be legal."

"Some of us get lucky like that." Sarah winked when I looked at her.

All of them—Rob, Tyler and Sarah—had inherited their mother's addiction, in one form or another. For Sarah, it had been alcohol, before she could even legally drink it, although now she was an addictions counselor. Rob had kicked his addiction to cocaine years ago. Tyler's drug of choice—and mine, soon after we met—had been heroin.

- 56 -

"You should see the photographs," Sarah said to me as Anne approached. She was wearing her signature combat boots with leggings and a t-shirt with a band I didn't know on it. "So many photographs! Mom, you have to show Katie—Tyler was so cute when he was little."

"You all were," Leanne said, watching her grandkids playing under the piano, a wistful look on her face.

"I'd love to see them," I told her, suddenly enamored with the idea of seeing Tyler as a baby. I hadn't even known pictures of him existed as a child. He'd lived a lot of his years in foster care, and all that had survived were standard school photos.

"You come over this week," Leanne said. "I'll call you."

"That would be great." I looked up as Sabrina came over to join the gaggle of girls—we'd all congregated together, while the guys were in another corner.

"Did I hear something about baby pictures?" Sabrina asked. "Do you have baby pictures of Rob?"

"I'll trade you, for some baby pictures of those two," Leanne offered, a glint in her eye. Sabrina laughed and said it was a deal—she just had to promise not to tell Rob.

Celeste and Daisy came over, too, to complete the gender segregation.

"Who are we waiting on?" I asked Celeste, assuming, rightly, that she would know.

"Arnie." Celeste sipped her wine, making a face. "He had a meeting. He said he's on his way."

Arnie was almost always late. Trouble's agent—now Sabrina's agent, too—had been singlehandedly responsible for putting Trouble together. He'd discovered Rob first, and together they'd found Tyler, still living in foster care. The other three Trouble members had been hand-picked by Arnie, although I couldn't understand it. There didn't seem to be any rhyme or reason to Jon, Nick and Kenny's addition to the band. Sure, they could play, but that was about it.

"I'm hungry," I apologized, getting up off the sofa. "And I don't get Daisy's food enough anymore."

"Don't miss out," Sabrina agreed, nodding toward the platters of appetizers. "She's in fine form tonight."

Before Tyler and I had bought our own place, we'd eaten Daisy's food every day. It was the thing I missed most about living with Rob and Sabrina—that, and the fact that we'd always had dinner together, depending on our schedules. Sarah had lived with Rob, then, too, so it really was like "family dinner." We tried to recreate that, now, once a month on a weekend, so we could catch-up.

I filled my plate with appetizers—hummus and deviled eggs and some sort of pinwheel pastry with salmon—and the crawled under the piano to check on Jay.

"Hey girlie," I said, offering her the plate.

"Oh yum." She took a deviled egg—the inside was green, and I suspected it was avocado—and wolfed it down. "Daisy made me a grilled cheese sandwich, but I'm still starving."

"Her grilled cheese is legendary around here," I said, through a mouthful of appetizer. "How are you, Jay?"

"I'm good, now," she said, tucking her long, dark hair behind her ears—out of Lucy's reach as she toddled toward Jay. The teen's hair was so black, it was almost blue, and it hung down past her waist.

"How did you get here?" I sat cross-legged, smiling as Henry crawled into my lap. "Did you really hitch a ride the whole way?"

"Yeah." Jay shrugged one thin shoulder.

I shook my head. "So dangerous. Why didn't you just call me?"

"I don't know." Jay rolled the ball and Lucy squealed and ran after it. "I guess… I just wanted out of there. And I thought, if I showed up here…"

Her voice trailed off and she shrugged again. I knew what she wasn't going to say—she thought if she showed up here, it would be harder for us to turn her away. And she was right, of course. Now she was here, and we were going to be forced to decide, one way or another.

"Arnie's here," I heard Jesse say, and I knew, once he'd settled in, Tyler would have to make his announcement.

"Come on," I said to Jay, edging my way out from under the piano. "It's almost time."

Jay blinked at me, looking confused, but she followed, crawling out from under, too. Lucy and Henry both followed her, Henry crawling and Lucy toddling. I caught Sabrina's eye—Mama Bear was keeping a good eye on them, even from a distance—and smiled.

I went over to join the group of women sitting on and around the sofa, but Jay veered off to fill a plate full of food. Lucy hugged her mother's legs for a moment, sucking her thumb and looking around like she wasn't quite sure about all of these people in her house. I watched Leanne playing silent peekaboo with her, both of them laughing.

The guys were saying hello to Arnie, and I heard Arnie reprimanding Tyler for taking off after his rumored "announcement." Tyler laughed and told Arnie he'd done worse—and Arnie agreed, laughing, too. Arnie had indeed spun a hell of a lot worse, I thought. He was the ultimate spin doctor.

Although sometimes the public was stubborn. It had been a long road getting them to accept Sabrina in Rob's life. I think part of it was Catherine's influence. Rob's ex was a model, like a blonde, blue-eyed angel, and while they'd been separated when he met Sabrina, the public didn't seem to care. They saw what they wanted to see.

Sabrina was an interloper, and Catherine was the victim.

It was only after Catherine showed her true colors—her attempt on Rob's life had gone awry, injuring Sabrina—that the public finally started to be swayed. After Catherine had been put away, Arnie had worked hard to push Sabrina into her place, to make the two of them live up to their couple nickname—Robalina.

The tide really started to turn when Sabrina lost Esther—their first baby. Then, when Lucy had been born, it was like some jubilant celebration in the press, a real victory. Arnie had given *People* the scoop, letting them do a photo shoot of the young couple and their newborn.

It was quite brilliant, on his part, given the darkness that had plagued all of us after Catherine decided to get back at Rob the only way she could, from inside the mental institution—telling the press the truth about their past. As much of it as she knew, anyway.

I still hated Catherine for what she'd done—for hurting Sabrina, and then, for revealing Rob, Tyler and Sarah's dark secrets. But Catherine had been a victim, too. It was hard to keep that out in front of me, when I thought about her, but it was true. She'd been just a child herself, back then, when their paths had first crossed.

"Peekaboo!" Leanne laughed, playing the game with Henry, now.

I could see the family resemblance, in spite of the scars on her face. She'd paid a big price for her addiction. Maybe more than any of us. Leanne had been the only adult alive back then who could have protected them all—Rob, Tyler, Sarah, even Catherine—but she'd been so entrenched in her addiction, she'd never taken that step.

When Catherine—just fifteen then—had announced she was leaving, Leanne's husband had refused to let her go. She was one of his "special" girls. The thought, even now, made me physically ill just to think about. Leanne had turned a blind eye to her husband's proclivities, because while Joe was running a child prostitution ring, he was also providing her with as much crack as she could ever want.

- 61 -

I don't know what made Leanne finally stand up and say no that day. I had never asked her—and I probably never would. But Catherine had wanted to leave, and Leanne had defended her, and that had started a snowball rolling downhill that would run over everyone in its path. It would lead to Joe's death—ten-year-old Tyler had shot the bullet that killed his father, while Joe had Leanne in a stranglehold—Leanne's arrest, and Rob, Tyler and Sarah's placement in foster care.

It would be years before they were reunited again. Years before Rob found and married Catherine. Years before their mother was released from jail, and finally put the last piece of the puzzle in place, telling them that Joe wasn't their father after all. Joe had no interest in women—he liked girls, the younger the better. He found them and groomed them, but he wasn't the one in charge.

The whole show was actually being run by Dante Marotta—the man Leanne was involved with, the one who had fathered three children with her. A man who would later become prosecutor for the state of California, who would also threaten the lives of those three children, once Catherine had made their "secret" public.

He was in jail now—along with several other public figures that could be linked to one of the largest child prostitution rings in the country—and couldn't hurt any of us anymore. But for a while there, after the scandal was made public, we all worried if Trouble had finally run into the sort of trouble they would just never be able to recover from.

It was Arnie who had saved them, I thought, watching the portly, balding little man talking and laughing with the band. He wasn't much to look at—especially in juxtaposition to stars like Rob and Tyler—but he was better at his job than anyone I'd ever known. He was like a magician. He could spin anything into gold. He'd created Trouble from nothing, and then he'd managed to keep them out of trouble, in spite of the incredible scandal that had plagued them.

He'd turned Rob into a hero. It had been Tyler who pulled the trigger—but Rob who had taken the fall. Tyler's older brother had taken advantage of Ty's mute shock after the incident, and had confessed to the crime. Twelve-year-old Rob had spent time in juvy, but given the circumstances, his punishment hadn't been too severe. And when Catherine told the press, she'd wanted to hurt Rob and his image, so that's the story she told.

No one, aside from us, knew that it had been Tyler who pulled the trigger. The press had run with Catherine's story, and Arnie had taken advantage of it to make Rob into some sort of young hero, a boy who had been abused by his father, who had killed the man who was trying to strangle his mother.

Arnie could spin anything. Now "Robalina" was the darling of the press, with their perfect family. Rob was the ultimate reformed "bad boy." Even the girls who swooned over him and wanted to marry him—like young Jay, who had been so enamored with him at the age of twelve, she'd snuck on a tour bus to meet him—couldn't help loving Sabrina. She was beautiful, an amazing singer, and she and Rob were so much in love, it was like a light around them. Add two adorable babies to that mix, and the press couldn't resist. They loved them all.

And Arnie had been behind the whole thing, orchestrating. He would feign surprise tonight, when Tyler made his announcement—but Arnie already knew about Tyler's diagnosis. Tyler had told him, before asking Arnie to find him more dramatic roles. Arnie was smart, shrewd—I thought he'd been planning for this day for a while now, pushing Tyler into acting while raising Sabrina's popularity in the press.

I watched Tyler, who seemed so at ease, smiling, laughing, but I wondered if anyone else saw the muscle working in his jaw, the way his shoulders tensed whenever anyone clapped him on the back. This wasn't going to be easy for him. I didn't blame him for saying he was only going to make this announcement once.

I made my way over to Tyler, putting an arm around his waist, and he smiled down at me, but that tension was still there. He didn't want to do this— and I wished he didn't have to. It seemed like some cruel twist of fate, to give a man such an incredible talent, only to curse him with a disease that would make it impossible for him to use it.

Rob went over to the piano and playing something—I only half-recognized it, but it got everyone's attention—and then ceded the floor to his brother. Tyler's announcement was brief and heartbreaking. I stood by his side the whole time, and I think I was the only one who knew he was trembling just slightly as he told them all he wouldn't be playing guitar in the band anymore. And he finally told them why.

Leanne listened with tears rolling down her cheeks. Sarah and Anne clung to each other, both of them crying silently. Sabrina dabbed her eyes with a Kleenex. Even Daisy, who was taking an empty platter back to the kitchen, stopped to listen, her eyes welling with tears.

The guys were simply stunned. Rob, of course, already knew. Arnie acted shocked and sad—a perfect acting job. I didn't cry, but Tyler's revelation was so heavy it felt like, if his arm hadn't been there around my waist to hold me up, I would have collapsed under its weight.

Leanne got up to hug Tyler and tell him how sorry she was—and everyone had an opinion about treatment and doctors and possible solutions. But Tyler was resolute. He was leaving the band. That was final.

"What the hell are we going to do?" Nick asked. He was back on the sofa with Jon and Kenny— they'd sunk down together at the news, like their legs wouldn't even hold them up anymore. I knew just how they felt.

"We'll find another lead guitarist," Arnie said, waving their concern away. "I found you three, didn't I?"

Some discovery, I thought, but didn't say, hiding a smirk in Tyler's shoulder.

Then Jay piped up—she was sitting on the floor by the sofa, holding Henry in her lap.

"Why doesn't Sabrina join the band?"

I winced, waiting for the "three stooges" to object. They'd never liked Sabrina—even though the tide had turned for her in the press. They looked at her like Trouble's Yoko Ono, afraid she was going to take Rob—their big meal ticket—away.

But Arnie spoke up before they could. "Best idea I've heard yet."

"Thanks!" Jay beamed up at him.

"Who is this brilliant, beautiful young lady?" Arnie asked, cocking his head and looking at her. Even in jeans and a t-shirt, Jay was a fresh, stunning beauty. I saw Arnie looking at her with "agent" eyes and groaned inwardly.

"My cousin," I lied, feeling Tyler looking at me. Since I'd already lied to his mom, I decided to just keep up the ruse, even though Rob and Sabrina knew who she really was. "Jay, this is Arnie, Tyler's agent."

"Jay?" Arnie's smile widened. "She's already got a model's name. You should come see me. I can get a modeling job for you in a heartbeat."

"Really?" Jay's eyes widened, and she took Arnie's offered card with reverence. "Me? A model?"

"You want Sabrina to join the band?" Nick asked, changing the subject back to the one at hand. "Are you kidding me? Didn't you say the label didn't want her?"

Arnie shrugged. "That was before she had proved she could sell records. And now that she's done having babies and she's got her figure back? I think we could really make it work…"

"Dude, if anyone can make it work, it's you," Rob told him, putting an arm around his wife's shoulders. Sabrina looked a little stunned, but she had to have known that this was a possibility. Maybe she was still reeling from Arnie's "figure" comment—he'd never been nice about Sabrina's curves.

Soon they were all talking about the possibility, and somehow Tyler's tragic announcement had been forgotten. Celeste came over to hug him and tell him how sorry she was—but I think she already knew, at least suspected. She'd been the one who got us a doctor on the road who had given Tyler his shots that had helped, at least for a little while. Along with the truckload of Vicodin he was taking at the time.

"I've got to put these two down for a nap," Sabrina announced, taking a fussy Henry from Jay. "Do you want to help me?"

Jay was ecstatic at that and followed Sabrina upstairs. Tyler and I sat on the couch with his mother, who was still talking with Anne and Sarah. Sarah was still exclaiming over the baby pictures they found.

"You didn't tell me about your grandmother," I said, nudging Tyler.

"Oh, sorry..." He frowned. "Sarah called me just before we left, and... I guess I didn't want to spoil our vacation."

"Do you remember her at all?" I asked.

"Vaguely." Tyler shrugged, looking over at his mother. "I... I don't remember a lot from that time."

I nodded, putting my head on his shoulder. He'd spent his first year in foster care not speaking at all.

They called him an "elective mute." He'd come out of it eventually—Tyler said it was music, really, that had saved him. He'd thrown himself into playing guitar and writing songs. It had been his calling, even then.

The thought of him never playing again broke my heart.

"You need to see the baby pictures," Sarah insisted. "Ty, you were so adorable. All that blonde hair!"

"I'd love to see them," I said again, watching as Jay came down the stairs with Sabrina. The babies had obviously gone down easily for their nap.

"Maybe you can come over for dinner this week, Mom," Tyler suggested. "We've got Jay with us... but I don't know for how long..."

"Indefinitely," I said, putting my hand in his and squeezing. I heard him sigh.

"So this little morsel is staying with you?" Arnie interrupted, coming over just as Jay settled on the floor by the sofa. "Where in the world have you been hiding her, Katie? This face belongs on billboards and in magazines, I'm telling you."

"Arnie," I warned, rolling my eyes. "She's only fifteen.

"Look at that face." Arnie ignored me, smiling down at Jay. "That's the face that could launch a thousand ships."

"Hey." I snapped my fingers, getting Arnie's attention. "Get the dollar signs out of your eyes. She's not becoming a model."

"Why not?" Jay piped up.

"Yeah, why not?" Arnie grinned at me.

- 68 -

"Okay, Ty, I think we should go." I stood, looking down at Jay. "We need to get her settled. And I'm still jetlagged."

Tyler didn't argue with me, and we said our goodbyes, finding Jesse in the kitchen with Celeste and Daisy. Our luggage was still in the back of the Rolls. Leanne left with us, and so did Sarah and Anne, since they were her ride. I didn't blame her for not wanting to stay, considering the babies were in bed, and Rob hadn't been too keen on her being there in the first place.

"I can't wait to see those baby pictures," I said, giving Leanne a hug.

Leanne hugged Tyler, too, then she hugged Jay, who looked surprised.

"You stay in school," Leanne told Jay, holding her chin in her hand and looking into her eyes. "Trust me, hon—even if beauty isn't stolen from you, like it was from me—it always fades. You can't rely on it forever. Stay in school and find something you love to do. Okay?"

"O—okay." Jay nodded, blinking in surprise.

We got into the Rolls and Jesse circled around and started up the long driveway toward the gate. Jay settled between us in the backseat, her backpack between her feet. It was the only thing she'd brought with her from home, the poor thing.

I felt Tyler's hand on my shoulder and glanced over at him, seeing the same exhaustion on his face. What a day it had been—what a freaking day.

"I love you," I mouthed over Jay's head as she snuggled against me, closing her eyes. Tyler looked down at her, his gaze softening. The way he looked at her was sweet, concerned. Almost fatherly. It made my ovaries ache.

"What happened to her face?" Jay asked, her eyes still closed. "Was she in a fire?"

"My father burned it," Tyler said, meeting Jay's stare when her eyes flew open at his words. "He held her face to a stove—to 'teach her a lesson,' or so he said."

"Really?" Jay breathed, looking at me for confirmation. I nodded. It had been Dante who had done that, to terrorize all of them, to keep them from telling his dirty secrets.

"Jeez." Jay shuddered, pressing against me again. "And I thought I had it bad."

"I'm sorry," Tyler said softly, but Jay was already drifting off.

I didn't even know what time it was, but I was exhausted, too. I saw the concern on Tyler's face as he looked from Jay, up to me. He wanted to know— *what are we going to do with her?*

What are we going to do? `

But I didn't know. We would have to figure it out, but right then, I just wanted to get my little family home and take a long, long nap.

So that's just what we did.

Chapter Five

"But my mom lets me drink coffee all the time at home," Jay protested as we got in line at Starbucks. "Lattes, mochachinos…"

"Yeah, and your mom let you go to a Trouble concert by yourself when you were twelve, too," I reminded her, handing over a twenty. "Decaf only. Got it?"

"Fine." Jay rolled her eyes and sighed in true teen fashion, and I managed to hide my smile before going to find us a table.

I saw Sabrina struggling with the door and waved. I would have gone to help her, but a guy in bike shorts pushed the door from the inside, holding it open to let her wheel the double stroller in. Lucy was in front, and squealed loudly when she saw me, turning several head. Henry was in back, sucking on a sippy-cup.

"What do you want?" I asked as Sabrina parked the stroller beside the table, but out of the aisle. "I can tell Jay."

"Uhhh… just a white hot chocolate," she said, making a face. "I'm still nursing Henry and I don't want to do any coffee. Even the decaf has some caffeine."

"It does?" I asked in surprise, looking over at Jay. This whole parenting thing wasn't exactly easy, and I'd only been doing it for a week. I went over to give Jay another twenty, telling her what to order for Sabrina.

"You should get a hot chocolate, too," I advised. "Did you know that even decaf coffee has some caffeine in it?"

"It's not like it's going to stunt my growth," Jay said, rolling her eyes yet again. "I'm already five-seven."

"Jay." I'd perfected that warning 'Mom' tone already. In under a week. Of course, I'd learned everything I needed to know from my own mother, who I found coming out of my mouth more than I ever thought possible this week.

"Fine!" She tucked both twenties in her cleavage—where she had stashed the iPhone we got for her. This was another thing I didn't like, the storing of electronics in her bra. It had to contribute to breast cancer, I argued. But I'd learned, even just in a week's time, to pick my battles.

"So how's it going with her?" Sabrina asked as I slid into my chair at the table. She had Lucy out of the stroller on her lap, but Henry seemed content to lean back with his sippy cup.

"Jay?" I shrugged, looking fondly at the girl standing in line. Several guys had done a double take when they passed her by, and I gritted my teeth at that. "She's great. We love having her."

That was mostly true. Really, she wasn't that bratty. She was mostly sweet, and helpful, if sometimes a little moody. Compared to most teens I knew—heck, compared to the teenage I'd been—she was an angel. And considering what she'd run away from at home, she was doing fantastic.

- 72 -

"But what are you going to do with her?" Sabrina asked, narrowing her eyes in Jay's. "You're going to have to make a decision… sooner rather than later."

"Yeah." I sighed. Tyler kept saying that, too. Her mother would be looking for her, wouldn't she? She'd probably filed a police report.

"I mean, before we start seeing her face on the side of milk cartons?" Sabrina prompted.

"I know, I know." I smiled when Lucy reached for me and I took her from Sabrina, settling her in my lap. "I just… I want her to get settled. Let things calm down a little…"

"Maybe she shouldn't get so settled?" Sabrina frowned over at Jay. "I mean, she's a runaway. She's crossed state lines. I'm not a lawyer, but if I was, I'm pretty sure I'd be advising you that keeping a runaway in your house without telling her mother is a bad idea…"

"Her mother doesn't care," I insisted, bouncing Lucy on my knee. "I don't even know if she'll even bother with a missing person's report."

"She'll care if she finds out where Jay is," Sabrina said knowingly. "If that mother finds out her underage daughter is living with a rock star? Who has a boatload of money? All of a sudden, she'll care a whole lot."

"Yeah." I made a face as Lucy reached for the silverware sitting on the table. I pushed it out of her reach and she protested. It was easier keeping the little ones out of trouble, I thought, glancing up to see Jay at the head of the line. I decided to change the subject before she came back to the table. "Hey, so I saw you and Rob and the babies on TMZ."

"Arnie's idea." Sabrina shook her head, wiping a spoon with a napkin and handing it to Lucy to play with. "He's pushing it out slowly in the press... letting them get used to it."

"They love you," I told her. "And the babies. The whole world loves you guys now. They'll love you in Trouble."

"I just wish Tyler didn't have to quit." She looked at me, and I saw the sadness in her eyes. "They're crucifying him in the press."

"He's fine with it," I said with a shrug.

While the media had already warmed up to the idea of Sabrina joining Trouble, printing all sorts of speculation, they'd vilified Tyler. Rumors were flying, judgements being made. It was all over the internet, op-ed pieces and comments on articles—he was selfish, he thought he was too good for Trouble now that he was acting, he wanted more money, he wanted to be the front man—you name it, they'd said it.

But Tyler wouldn't budge. He'd refused all interviews, and he wouldn't let them know the real reason he'd quit. *It'll blow over*, was all he'd say, and I knew he was right. Eventually, it would blow over. But would we still be standing when it did?

"I doubt he's 'fine' with it," Sabrina said softly.

"Well..." I shifted Lucy in my lap, seeing Jay balancing a drink holder as she approached. "I guess 'fine' isn't the right word. Resigned, maybe. He's accepted it. What else can he do?"

"I guess." She gave a sad sigh, looking up as Jay slid into the empty chair at the table.

"White hot chocolate for you." Jay put a cup in front of Sabrina, turning to put a cup in front of me. "Grande skinny caramel macchiato for you. And another white hot chocolate for me."

"Good girl." I winked at her and she rolled her eyes, but she smiled behind her cup. I think she secretly liked the fact that I sweated the small stuff like caffeine and keeping tabs on her every minute of the day.

Lucy squirmed in my lap, trying to crawl across the table to Jay. They hadn't seen each other since Tyler's announcement, but clearly Lucy remembered her. Jay laughed and held her arms out. I put Lucy on the floor and she toddled around the table to sit in Jay's lap.

"Wish I could find a nanny she liked as much." Sabrina blew steam off the top of her hot chocolate, watching Lucy and Jay together. "Remember that psycho we had on the road last year?"

"I remember," I told her. "I was the one who picked up the slack after you fired her."

"I guess I'm spoiled." Sabrina gave a dirty look to a woman with a laptop at the table next to us. Lucy was laughing and squealing and banging a spoon on the table, and the woman looked like she wanted to wring the little girl's neck. "With Daisy and Jesse and Celeste—we have such good help."

"It's the main reason I never get around to hiring anyone," I said with a laugh. "Who could live up to Daisy's cooking?"

"Right?" Sabrina reached over to unbuckle Henry's belt, taking him out of the stroller just as he was starting to fuss.

"Ohh snap." I sank lower in my chair, seeing who was coming through the door. "That's her."

"Her who?" Sabrina craned her neck to see past the line of people.

"Alisha McKenna." I sank a little lower, as if that could keep her from seeing me.

"That reporter?" Sabrina had located her and her eyebrows went up. "The Variety one?"

"Yup." She'd seen me—her fingers were waggling in my direction. Ugh.

"Well look who's here." Alisha slipped through the crowd, arriving at our table. I sat up straighter, since she'd already spotted me. "Where's your other half?"

I shrugged, not saying anything to her, taking a sip of my coffee. It was way too hot and I burned my tongue, but I pretended I hadn't.

"So it's really true then?" Alisha smoothed her obviously-dyed red hair behind her ears. She was dressed for work, which must have been paying her well, given the Jimmy Choos she was wearing. "Tyler Cook is leaving Trouble?"

"You should know," Sabrina snapped. "You were the one who printed it first."

"Tell Tyler I missed him this week at the studio." Alisha ignored Sabrina's laser-beam look, focusing on me. "Have him call me to reschedule."

I glared at her, ignoring the implication. I seriously doubted Tyler had arranged a meeting with Alisha McKenna. He knew how I felt about her— especially after what she'd printed, after he'd asked her not to.

"Come on," Alisha wrinkled her freckled nose at me. "You know I'll treat him right. Why don't you put in a good word for me?"

"The only word we've got for you, sweetheart, is 'no'." Sabrina waved her away, dismissing her presence and turning back to me. "So are you taking Jay shopping?"

"Yes!" Jay's face lit up. "New clothes—I can't wait!"

"So who's this, then?" Alisha's reporter instincts came out like a cat's claws. I could practically see her sniffing the air, trying to catch the scent of a rumor to start.

"My cousin." That was the story we'd be sticking to.

"Hm." Alisha cocked her head at Jay, her eyes narrowing slightly. "She's gorgeous."

"Thanks." Jay laughed, tickling Lucy, making her squeal with laughter, garnering another dirty look from laptop-lady.

"You don't look anything alike." Alisha slung her Gucci bag over her shoulder, sending her offhand barb straight through me. I didn't even answer her, pretending it didn't bother me in the least. "Tell Tyler I said 'hi.' I'm sure I'll see him around."

"Bitch," Sabrina said under her breath as Alisha flung her red hair over her shoulder and turned to go. I know Alisha heard her, but she didn't react, going over to stand in line for coffee. Sabrina looked at Jay and offered her a smile. "She's right though—you are gorgeous."

"Thanks." Jay wrinkled her nose at the compliment. "Maybe you can tell Katie that. Arnie gave me his card, but she won't let me call him."

"Do you really want to be a model?" Sabrina asked. "Be careful what you wish for."

"Sounds good to me," Jay said with a shrug. "What girl wouldn't want her face on Glamour?"

"Girls who like food." Sabrina laughed.

"You should see her eat." I snorted. "Jay eats more than I do."

"Must be nice to have that metabolism." Sabrina sighed. "So where are you taking her shopping? I'm so jealous. I haven't been shopping in ages. Hard to try anything on with these two."

"K-Mart." I laughed when Sabrina choked on her hot chocolate. "Just kidding. We'll probably hit Neiman Marcus and Macy's."

"Wish I could come." Sabrina sighed, shifting Henry to her other side, away from the narrowing gaze of laptop-lady. "But I've got to get these two down for a nap."

"You really do need a nanny." I caught the spoon sliding across the table that Lucy tossed my way.

"If you know any, give them my number." Sabrina gave Henry his sippy cup, which he happily accepted. His smile was so cute, with just his top and bottom two teeth in.

"I could do it." Jay caught Lucy's spoon before it sailed onto the floor. "I mean—I'm good with kids."

"You'll have school in the fall," I reminded her, catching Sabrina's frown. She didn't like me thinking that far ahead for Jay, especially out loud. I knew we were going to have to something more permanent at some point. Sooner rather than later. But for now, I just wanted to make sure Jay was safe and had the basics with us, before taking any bigger steps.

My phone buzzed and I dug it out of my purse, seeing Tyler's name on the screen. I held up my finger to Sabrina and Jay, taking the call.

"Hey sexy." Tyler's voice caressed me through the phone and I smiled, turning my face away from the table. "I got a surprise for you."

"You do?" I lowered my voice a little, glancing over to see Alisha watching us. "A good surprise?"

"I think so." He laughed. "Buy something sexy when you're out shopping with Jay. I'm taking my wife out to dinner."

"You are?" I blinked, watching Jay playing hide-the-spoon with Lucy. "But... uh... what about..."

"See if Jay can spend the night with Sabrina and Rob," he suggested, already anticipating my question. "If you don't want to leave her home alone."

"Okay," I agreed. I didn't think Sabrina would really mind, given the circumstances. She'd likely be grateful for the break. "Can you give me a hint?"

"Not even a little one." He chuckled.

"But it's good?"

"Yeah. Real good."

I smiled. "At least tell me where we're going to dinner."

"Spago."

"Spago? Really? Beverly Hills? It must be *really* good news."

"I want you to wear something super-sexy." He lowered his voice. "Something I won't be able to wait to take off you."

His words made my whole body flush with heat.

"You got it. What time tonight?"

"Reservations at eight. I'll be home by seven to shower."

"How's the read-through going?"

"Good," he said. "In fact, I gotta get back. See you tonight, sexy."

"Mmkay." I slipped my phone back into my purse, seeing both Jay and Sabrina looking at me. "What?"

"Spago, huh?" Sabrina raised her eyebrows.

"He says he's got a surprise." I shrugged one shoulder, sipping my coffee—it had cooled down enough I could drink it now—but it was hard not to smile. "Good news."

"We could use some good news." Sabrina looked over at Jay. "Hey, sweetie, how would you like to spend the night at our place? A little audition for that nanny position?"

Jay brightened, looking at me. "Could I?"

"Sure," I agreed, smiling my thanks at Sabrina. She'd either read my mind—or she'd overheard at least some of what Tyler had said. "I can drop her off after we go shopping, if that works for you?"

"Perfect." Sabrina nodded, watching Jay with Lucy. "I can't wait to hear the good news."

"Me, either."

I was both excited and nervous—my imagination was running wild with the possibilities—but the thought of dinner out with my husband, and more importantly, surprising him by wearing something short and low-cut and impossible to resist, took precedence.

It was definitely time to go shopping.

"I am going to tear that off you and fuck you right on this table." Tyler murmured in my ear. I didn't say anything as the maître d' sat us at an out-of-the-way booth in the corner, but my belly quivered when I saw the dark look of lust in my husband's eyes as I slid into my seat.

I rapped my knuckles on the table, glancing over at him. "Seems sturdy enough."

"Don't tempt me."

I smirked, opening my menu while Tyler ordered wine.

Shopping that afternoon had been a resounding success. Jay had a whole new wardrobe. I'd gone a little overboard, but I figured, even if I had to send her home, she wouldn't go empty-handed. She was fun to shop for, and I'd appreciated having someone besides the salesgirl telling me which dress I should or shouldn't settle on for my date night with Tyler.

Jay had helped me get ready—in the guest bathroom, so I could surprise my husband with the big reveal. He came home to shower, calling for me, but I sent Jay out to tell him I was busy getting ready. The dress looked like it was painted on. It was designer—Versace—a dark blue that was almost black, with a sort of silver lace overlay. It was almost entirely backless, and the hemline came to just above my knee.

For as much as it cost, it wasn't much material—but it had a very satisfying impact when I came down the stairs wearing silver heels and carrying a little silver clutch to complete the ensemble. If Jay hadn't been there, I don't think we would have made it out of the house at all, given the hungry look in Tyler's eyes.

"Sufficient?" I'd inquired innocently, smiling when he growled and grabbed me, kissing me hard and long, right in front of Jay.

Tyler drove the Mustang convertible—Jay's car request—dropping her off at Sabrina and Rob's with an overnight bag before we headed to the restaurant. The night was warm, but my dress didn't cover much. Tyler's hand on the bare skin of my lower back, guiding me into the restaurant, was a promise of the night to come.

"So what's the surprise?" I asked him as we sipped wine and waited for dinner.

"If I have to wait to get you out of that dress, you can wait for the surprise." He smirked at me when I stuck out my tongue.

Dinner was amazing, but Tyler laughed when I told him in hushed tones that Daisy's food was better.

"Don't tell Wolfgang Puck that," Tyler said, stealing a spoonful of my sorbet. We weren't exactly eating clean tonight, given the celebratory circumstances.

"Are you ever going to tell me?" I asked him over coffee. "Or are you just going to leave me hanging all night? The suspense is killing me."

"That dress is killing me." He sighed, leaning back against the booth, his gaze moving down the V that plunged between my breasts. I couldn't wear a bra, considering how backless it was—and underneath, I just had a pair of black panties and thigh-highs.

"Then take me home." I stirred cream into my coffee, watching it turn color. "We've got it all to ourselves for the first time in a week... I can be as loud as I want."

We'd gone from having to be quiet at my mother's, to now having to be quiet because Jay was sleeping down the hall. We weren't used to being quiet.

"I'm going to make you scream so loud," he promised, meeting my eyes, giving me a look so hot I thought I was going to melt into a puddle.

"Prove it," I challenged, waggling my eyebrows at him.

Tyler leaned forward—the elbows of his black button-down on the table. He was never the type to wear a suit—the last time I remembered him in one, it was our wedding day—but he'd was dressed up tonight, for Tyler. He was even wearing dress shoes—instead of Keds.

"What do you think of New Zealand?" he asked, cocking his head at me.

"Uhhhh." I blinked, then laughed. "I think it's where they filmed all the Lord of the Rings movies. It's very green. Right?"

"Yeah." He nodded, a half-smile on his face. "What would you think about living there?"

I couldn't breathe. "L...living there?"

- 83 -

"Well, not permanently or anything. Just for about six months."

"You got the part." My mouth went instantly dry and my hands shook as I tried to get my coffee cup to my mouth. I gulped, looking at Tyler's grinning face over the rim.

"It's perfect, Katie. *Album* will be on hiatus. We can move to New Zealand for six months, then come back so I can film the series."

"Of course, Peter Jackson wants to film it in New Zealand." I choked. I'd known, if Tyler got the part, that's where we'd have to go. But it had been so long since he'd auditioned for it, I hadn't really thought he was going to get it. So many other people had been up for the part.

"Are you happy?" He cocked his head, looking at me, hopeful.

"Oh Ty, I'm so happy for you!" I reached across the table and grabbed his hands, squeezing them in mine. They were still calloused from years of guitar-playing, and I rubbed them with my fingertips.

"For us." He turned my hands over, palms up, lifting one, then the other, so he could kiss the inside of my wrists. "For us, baby."

"I'm with you all the way," I told him. Then I swallowed, biting my lip to keep from saying anything else. But Tyler must have seen something on my face.

"What is it?" He held my hands, rubbing his thumbs over the sensitive skin of my inner wrists, making me shiver. "You were so excited about it, when I auditioned..."

"I was," I agreed. "I mean... I am. I just..."

"It's only six months," he reminded me.

"I know." I sighed. "But six months ago, we didn't have Jay."

"Jay." He sighed, too, shaking his head. "We really need to talk."

"About Jay?"

He nodded. "I uh... I had a conversation with Trouble's lawyer this week."

I looked at him but didn't say anything.

"Katie, we really could get into a lot of trouble, getting in the middle of this thing."

"We're already in the middle of it," I reminded him.

"I know you don't want to hear this... but I think we need to send her home."

"Home?" I sat back, pulling my hands out of his and putting them in my lap. "Ty... you don't know what you're saying. She can't go home."

"She's a minor," he said softly.

"But—"

"And until a judge says differently, she belongs at home with her family."

"But—"

"Katie, we can't keep her here." His words actually brought tears to my eyes. "I'm glad she had you to turn to, and I will do whatever I can to help her, but there's only so much we can do. Legally, I mean."

"So you want to send her home?" Something curled up in the pit of my stomach.

"I don't want to." He sighed. "But I think we have to."

I shook my head, denying it. I didn't want it to be true. I'd just bought her a whole wardrobe, in hopes that she'd wear her new clothes to school in the fall. I wanted to keep my head buried firmly in the sand when it came to facing the fact that Jay was a runaway, and I didn't have a clue how to solve that problem.

"I can't send her back to them." I spoke the words slowly, carefully. I was trying my best not to burst into tears in the middle of Spago. "What if... what if we send her back... and something happens to her?"

He sighed, hanging his head for a moment. Then he looked up at me. "I don't know, Katie. I want to help her. But... we're really walking on thin ice, here."

"Can't we try?" I sniffed, blinking back my tears. "I don't just want to send her back without... without trying..."

"What do you want to try, baby?" He leaned forward, frowning across the table at me.

"Can we at least go talk to a lawyer?" I pleaded. "See what our options are?"

"Yeah." He nodded slowly. "Sure. We can do that."

"Thank you." I met his eyes, seeing him through prisms. "It means the world to me. And to Jay."

"Anything for you, baby." He slipped out of the booth to come sit next to me on my side, putting an arm around my shoulders. "Don't worry. Somehow... we'll figure this out."

"Thank you," I said again, leaning into him. "I'm sorry, Ty. I'm so sorry. I didn't mean to spoil your surprise. I'm excited for you, I really am."

"You didn't spoil anything." He kissed the top of my perfectly-coiffed head—Jay had insisted on hot-rollers and then had swept all my honey-colored hair up into a configuration that looked sort of messy but was actually carefully arranged.

"New Zealand." I said it, trying to make it real. Six months away from everyone and everything I knew, in another country. I looked at him, letting it sink it. "This is huge. I mean—really, really huge."

"It is." He nodded. "If we were looking to really make a change, a great big door just opened."

"And all we have to do is go through it..." I smiled up at him.

"One step at a time." He leaned in to kiss me, his lips soft and full. Every time he kissed me, it was like everything else stopped. The whole world on its axis paused just for that moment. Nothing else mattered.

"Take me home," I whispered when we parted.

He nodded, his hand warm, electric, on the bare skin of my lower back. "Let's go."

Chapter Six

There was something extremely sexy about watching Tyler shift gears. He drove fast, which I loved, shifting as we wound our way up into the hills towards home. I'd only had a few glasses of wine, but my head felt light, and in spite of not knowing what we were going to do about Jay, I was also incredibly happy.

When I'd first discovered Tyler had decided to leave the band, part of me had panicked. What were we going to do without Trouble? Tyler's success on *Album* had been phenomenal—beyond our wildest dreams, really—but he played a 70s rock star. It was typecasting, sure—but could he sustain that level of success in a show that didn't showcase rock stars? I never would have said anything to him—but I worried.

Not that I didn't have confidence in him—I did. I think I had more confidence in him than he had in himself. He'd hesitated when Arnie told him about this audition, almost six months ago now. But I'd encouraged him. He didn't want to always play rock stars, did he? I'd encouraged him to audition, crossing my fingers—but we'd never heard back. Until now.

Now he'd been validated even more as an actor. He'd been cast in one of the biggest franchises in the movie business. Clearly someone with serious decision-making skills and power thought he could do it. I knew he could—he was on the precipice of truly breaking out, moving past Trouble and being thought of as "just a rock star."

I was so proud of him. I couldn't begin to express it fully. I put my hand over his as he shifted again, slowing the car as we neared our driveway. The car purred to a stop and he glanced over at me, giving me a wink as he rolled down the driver's side window and put in the security code that would open the gate.

"This is the beginning," I told him as he steered the car through the gates—they swung closed behind us—and up the winding drive. "Our whole lives are going to change."

"I know." He hit the garage door opener and it opened. Tyler had a collection of cars—half a dozen in all, not including his Harley and Valkyrie motorcycles—and he parked the Mustang at the end, in an empty spot next to the BMW I liked to drive.

"Are you scared?" I asked.

"Excited." He turned t0 look at me in the dim light. "And... relieved."

"Relieved?"

"I've been keeping it in, you know," he explained. "My diagnosis, and then whether or not I wanted to stay with Trouble. Now, finally...it's all out there."

"Yeah. The press is having a field day with it, though." I sighed, sliding my hand into his. "Hey, did you tell Alisha McKenna you'd do a follow-up interview with her about you leaving the band?"

"Who?" He laughed when I nudged him. "No, baby, I haven't talked to her. Although Celeste said she's being calling her non-stop."

- 89 -

"We saw her at Starbucks." I made a face. "She said she'd talked to you."

"And you believed her?" He smirked.

"Well, she is your type, isn't she?" I asked with a sniff. "Curvy redheads—that's what the guys on the tour bus always said."

"Once upon a time, I had a thing for redheads," he confessed. "Then I met this sassy, skinny blonde chick, and she chased all the other women out of my head."

"Is that so?" I turned towards him slightly and my dress rode up, revealing the lace top of my thigh-high.

"Very much so." His hand slid out of mine and settled on my knee, massaging slowly. His fingers were magical, sending hot little electrical impulses straight between my thighs. "I don't even see other women anymore. It's like they're not even there. All I see is you."

"You're such a liar," I teased, shifting in my seat and leaning toward him. I saw his gaze drop to my cleavage, saw the flash of heat in his eyes. "What's-her-name, your co-star on *Album*—she's hot. You have to admit, she's hot."

It had been a test of my sanity, watching his love scenes with her in *Album*. She kind of looked like me—long blonde hair, kind of slight—and Tyler once told me, he just closed his eyes and pretended it was me when he was kissing her.

"You're just trying to get me in trouble, aren't you?" He chuckled, his hand moving up under my dress. My breath caught in my throat when he cupped me through my panties and leaned in to kiss me. I gasped when his tongue touched mine, and his fingers slid under the elastic to pet my skin.

"Nope, you're officially not in Trouble, anymore," I reminded him when we parted, hearing him chuckle again as he nuzzled my bare neck. His mouth left hot, wet trails that made my nipples harden instantly.

"It's time for dessert," he whispered into my ear, his finger moving slowly inside of me, making me squirm.

"We had dessert at the restaurant…"

"Nuh-uh," he said, lifting the hand that had been between my legs to his mouth, sucking on his finger. "Nothing as sweet as this."

"You know, we have the whole house to ourselves," I reminded him with a little smile. "You know what that means…"

"It means I'm going to give my wife at least ten screaming orgasms."

"Ten?" I laughed. "That's quite a number."

"I'm up for the challenge." He waggled his eyebrows. "You?"

"Let's go find out."

When we'd first moved into this house, we'd been determined to christen every room in it—and we had. Even the bathrooms—all five of them. And the garage—in the back of the Mercedes, because it was roomier. Then we christened the patio out back.

Although we'd only had sex in the ocean a few times—because I swear, sand was impossible to get out of all those little cracks and crevices you didn't even think about, until you got sand in them. I told

Tyler, after the last time we'd had sex on the beach, that I understood the pain of oysters.

So we didn't stop in the foyer, or on the stairs. We went straight to our bedroom—Tyler went into our bathroom, and I lit a few candles and slipped off my heels.

"Don't you dare take off that dress!" Tyler called from behind the bathroom door.

"You better hurry up then," I called back, sitting on the edge of the bed. "Because I just might start withou—"

The bathroom door flew open and Tyler stormed out, growling at me, and I giggled, holding my arms out for him.

"Mine," he insisted, edging his way between my thighs and kissing me, his hands moving through the mass of my hair. Bobby pins went everywhere—not that I cared. "I've been thinking about doing this all night long."

He kissed my dress off. Every last inch of it, every bit of material that slipped off my body was followed by the hot, wet trail of his mouth. By the time he had me stripped down to my panties and thigh-highs, I was panting and desperate for him.

He had me just where he wanted me.

"Ty," I begged, but he rolled me to my belly and made me wait some more. My thigh highs came down first, one at a time, and he spent an inordinate amount of time licking behind my knees, making me squirm.

"Please," I moaned into the mattress, but then my panties had to come off. He rolled me over for that, easing them down and kissing all around my pubis, but never once parting me with his tongue.

I was delighted to find that, while he'd been undressing me, he had undressed himself. I reached for him, running my hands over his shoulders, down his belly, but he shifted away when I reached between his legs.

"Ty!" I protested, eager for him. "You bastard!"

"Yes, I am." He grinned, grabbing my wrists and pinning them above my head. "I love making you wait for it."

"So mean," I whispered against his lips as he kissed me. "You torture me…"

"Sweet torture," he countered, and I moaned when I felt his cock riding up and down the seam of my sex.

"Yes," I agreed, biting at his lip, lifting my hips, trying to nudge him inside me. "Come on, baby— stop teasing me."

"You want that?" His eyes grew dark as he rubbed his length up and down. "You want me inside you?"

"Yes!" I cried, my nails digging into his biceps. "Oh fuck, Ty!"

He finally gave me what I'd been begging for, with one delicious shift of his hips. I took his full length, moaning when he started to move. He wasn't teasing me anymore, and I was already so far gone, I was instantly on edge.

"That's it," he whispered into my ear, curling himself around me, thrusting deeper, harder, as I wrapped my legs around his waist. "That's my Katie… give it to me…"

"Ty!" I cried into the heat of his neck, licking the saltiness of his skin. "Oh God! Oh God!"

"Give it to me," he insisted, grunting with every thrust. "Oh fuck, yes, give it to me."

"Ohhhh now!" I cried, my pussy beginning to spasm, contracting around his plunging length. My climax seared through me, something hot and electric that made me quiver all over and buck underneath him.

"Mmmmm yeah," he groaned, nuzzling me, his breath coming hard and fast—but his cock was still hard and throbbing inside of me. "That's so damn hot."

"Your turn," I whispered, squeezing him with my muscles, hearing him moan softly.

"Nope." He propped himself up on his arms, grinning. "That was just one. At least nine more to go for you."

I laughed, but then he was pulling me out and turning me over, and I wasn't laughing anymore.

$$\text{♪}$$

"I think that's your phone."

"No." I shook my head, refusing to open my eyes as I snuggle up closer to Tyler under the comforter. "Shhhh."

All I wanted to listen to was the sound of Tyler's heart beating and the ocean waves on the beach outside. I loved it when we could sleep with the windows open. Then I heard it, too. A faint buzzing sound.

"Katie." He kissed the top of my head, his arms squeezing around me. "It's definitely your phone."

"Mmm." I sighed, still not opening my eyes. "Okay. In a minute. It's probably just my mom. She called yesterday and I haven't called her back."

"Oh, speaking of moms." Tyler's fingers moved lightly over my skin, petting my shoulder and upper arm, sending delightful little shivers through me. "Mine called, too."

"Oh yeah, she called me, too." I'd almost forgotten. "She wants to come over and bring those baby pictures."

Tyler snorted. "Oh great, you get to see me naked in the bathtub."

"Baby, I can see you naked in the bathtub whenever I want," I reminded him, sliding my hand down the ridges of his abdomen.

He chuckled. "Lucky you."

"Tell me about it." I smiled, tracing the dark line of hair running down from his navel. "Hey, you came up short, you know."

"Huh?"

"Ten screaming orgasms?" I reminded him. "I only counted six…"

"Who says we're done?" Tyler's hand moved under the covers, cupping my breast. He thumbed my nipple, making me gasp and open my eyes. Then I heard it again—my phone buzzing.

"I guess I should get that, before we start the engines again." I bit my lip, starting to slide across the mattress away from him.

"Oh no." He grabbed my hip, keeping me close. "I've got four more orgasms to give you first."

"First?" I laughed, trying to twist out of his grip. "But what if it's an emergency."

"Orgasm emergency, maybe." He grinned, lifting the edge of the comforter and diving underneath it.

I squealed, back-pedaling toward the pillows, but he grabbed my legs, yanking me back under the covers.

"Ty!" I cried, trying to wiggle away, but he held me fast, nipping at my thighs, soothing the nibbles with his tongue, working his way up toward my sex. I was still swollen and starting to get a little sore, but the feel of him between my legs made my pussy start to throb.

"Mmmm more dessert," he said, his voice muffled under the covers. "There's always room for Katie."

I laughed, squirming in his hold, knowing that fighting him was impossible. He was already parting my thighs, settling himself fully between them, and I moaned with his fingers found me.

"Ty," I said, biting my lip to keep from crying out when his tongue found me, too. "Oh God... wait... Ty... did you hear that?"

"Hear what?" His voice was muffled by more than just the covers now.

"I thought I heard a door. Downstairs."

Tyler's head appeared as he threw the covers back, his head cocked, listening. I listened, too, hoping I hadn't heard what I thought I had.

But now there were footsteps on the stairs.

"Jay." I looked at Tyler, feeling my heart lurch in my chest.

"I thought she was spending the night at Sabrina and Rob's?" He sat back on his heels, his gaze sweeping over me, completely naked on the bed, and I could almost read his thoughts.

"Something must have happened." I swung my legs off the bed, reaching for my robe, which was draped across a chair. "Maybe she got sick? Oh crap, I bet that was Sabrina on the phone."

"Come back." Tyler groaned, his voice muffled in a pillow now.

"I'll be right back." I promised, smiling back at him over my shoulder. "She probably just ate too much junk food. I'll get her some Pepto and tuck her in bed."

"Then come back and tuck me in." He rolled onto his side, propped up on his elbow. The covers fell across his hip and just looking at him made my mouth water.

"Promise," I promised, slipping out into the hallway.

We'd put Jay in a room down at the end of the hall—far enough away that I could have loud, if not screaming, orgasms, but not so far we couldn't hear her if she needed something. I saw her door shut and the light go on as I padded barefoot down the hall.

"Jay?" I called, knocking gently on the door. "Are you okay? Did you get sick?"

I waited for a response—I'd spent the week reading about teens, and "a sense of privacy" was apparently a big thing, and from my own not-so-distant teen years, I knew this was actually the case. I used to hate it when my mother would just walk into my room without knocking. Or, somehow even worse, knock briefly and then open the door without waiting for a response.

So I knocked again. "Jay? I just want to know you're okay."

"Go away!" Her voice was pillow-muffled. And it sounded like she'd been crying.

Crap.

"Jay... honey?" I cringed at my own invasion, but I turned the knob and eased the door open. "What is it?"

She was face-down on the bed, her hair in a long braid down her back—to keep it out of chubby, grasping baby-hands, I was sure—wearing a pair of her new jeans and a pretty, paisley peasant blouse. She was fifteen, but to me, she looked so little and vulnerable in the middle of that double bed.

"Are you all right?" I went over to sit on the edge of the bed beside her, putting a hand on her back. She flinched but didn't say anything. "Are you sick?"

"Yes." She nodded into the pillow, not pulling her face from it. "I'm sick. Very sick. Go away."

"Do you need anything?" I stroked her hair, smoothing the little flyaways down. "Some Tylenol? Pepto?"

"Noooo." She shook her head, sounding like she was holding back a sob. "Just... go away."

She took a deep breath and turned her face to the side, away from me. I could see mascara smudged on the pillowcase. Poor thing. She'd been crying.

"Please, Katie," she whispered. "Just go away. I want to sleep. Okay?"

"You sure?" I squeezed her shoulder. "I could get some ice cream. We could hang out and talk about... whatever..."

"Noooo!" She howled, turning her face into the pillow again. Her shoulders shook with silent sobs, and just watching her broke my heart.

"Okay," I relented, knowing now that whatever had happened, I was going to have to ask Sabrina. Jay wasn't going to tell me, at least not tonight. "Do you want me to turn the light out?"

"Yes, please." She sniffed as I went over to the door.

"If you need anything, we're right down the hall," I told her softly, flipping the switch to leave her in darkness. "Goodnight, Jay."

"G'nite," she whispered as I shut the door behind me.

I padded back down the hall and found Tyler sitting up in bed, his ear to his cell phone.

"Right. No, I get that. Of course." Tyler waved me in and I shut the door behind me, going to sit cross-legged on the bed beside him. "I totally understand... I will. Okay. Yep, I'll talk to you tomorrow."

Tyler tossed his phone on the bed and looked at me.

"Who was that?" I asked, although from the look on his face, I thought I already knew.

"Jay's no longer welcome over there." Tyler put his head in his hands for a moment, shaking it.

My heart dropped to my toes. "What happened?"

"What happened?" he repeated, looking at me, incredulous. Then he was up, stalking around the room. He grabbed a pair of jeans, yanking them on. "Holy fuck. I knew taking this girl in was a bad idea. Goddamnit, Katie…"

"What?" I asked again, watching him pull on a t-shirt. "What are you talking about?"

"Sabrina says she came onto Rob." He stopped the stalking when he got to our door, his hand on the knob.

I stared at him, aghast. "She... what?"

"You heard me." He pulled the door open and stormed down the hall.

I sat there for a moment, paralyzed, trying to make sense of his words. Jay came onto Rob? What did that mean, exactly? I mean, I knew she had a crush on him once upon a time. Rob was the reason Jay had finagled her way onto our tour bus. She had believed he was her "true love," and of course, thought that if she showed up, Rob would fall immediately in love with her.

But she'd been a kid then—just twelve, at the time. And her interests had grown since then. She still loved Trouble, but she wasn't obsessed with Rob Burns anymore. At least, that's what she'd told me, in emails, and during the conversations we had at least once a month.

Of course she told you that. If she told you she was still madly in love with him, would you have taken her in when she showed up on your doorstep?

"What in the hell were you thinking?" Tyler's voice boomed down the hallway and I leapt off the bed, heading after him. He was standing in Jay's doorway, the door open, light on. "Is that what you came here looking for? You wanted to fuck a rock star?"

"Tyler!" I called, horrified, as I hurried down the hall. "Tyler, don't!"

"Don't?" He turned to blink at me, incredulous. "Are you kidding me? This little slut shows up on our doorstep, we take her in, we buy her a whole goddamned new wardrobe, and how does she repay us?"

"Ty, stop," I whispered, seeing Jay sitting up on her bed, face in her hands, sobbing. "Let me talk to her."

"I'm done." Tyler held up his hands, glaring at Jay, and then at me. "I want her out of here. I want her on a plane tomorrow back to Kansas or Missouri or whatever rock she crawled out from under."

"Please." I put my hand on his arm. "Don't do this. I'll talk to her. I'll—"

"Whatever." Tyler turned and stalked back down the hall, slamming the door to our bedroom behind him. I knew why he was angry—and I couldn't blame him. If Jay really had come onto Rob, the way he said, then the fact that Jay was underage, and a runaway, put an even bigger wrench into the works. That was the sort of publicity Arnie would have a heart attack about -even he didn't have the power to spin that the right direction.

"Jay, what happened?" I asked, closing her door behind me and coming to sit by her on the bed.

"I'm so sorry, Katie," she whispered, lifting her head to look at me. Dark tracks, wet eyeliner and mascara, streaked her face. "It wasn't what it looked like. I didn't mean anything. Rob tried to tell her, but—"

Whatever she was going to say got choked off in a sob and Jay buried her face in her hands again. I moved to sit by her, putting an arm around her shoulder, and she turned to me, wrapping her arms around my neck.

"I ruin everything," she choked, her body shaking with sobs.

"No, you don't," I soothed. "You didn't. I'm sure it was just a misunderstanding. We'll fix it. In the morning, I promise, we'll fix it."

"But you heard him," Jay whispered. She was curled up against me, almost fetal. I rocked her like a baby, too, kissing the top of her head. "He wants me to go home."

"He's just... he doesn't know it was a mistake."

I closed my eyes, feeling tears sting them. I didn't know what had happened, but if Jay said it had been a misunderstanding, I believed her. I loved Sabrina dearly, but she did have a tendency to go overboard with the jealousy. She'd gone through several nannies because she thought they were coming on to Rob. Granted, some of them really had been—but she might have jumped the gun on one or two.

"I'm sorry, Katie, I'm so sorry," she said again. She was trembling, so I pulled her covers up, wrapping them around her. "But I can't go home... I can't... you don't know..."

"I know," I assured her.

"No, you don't!" she wailed, sobbing again. She cried so hard I thought it would tear her apart. I tried to calm her, and finally, she did settle down, her breath coming in hitches, like babies do after going on a crying jag.

"Here." I handed her a water bottle sitting on the night stand. "Drink this."

She did, sniffling and wiping at her face. Her nose was red and so were her eyes.

"Come on, lie down," I suggested, pulling the covers up and rolling her head ono a pillow. "Try to go to sleep. Things will be better in the morning."

"Lies." She sniffed, but half smiled, curling up with her back to my front. "Will you sing to me?"

"I can't sing," I said, stroking her damp cheek.

"I don't care." She closed her eyes, her breathing slower now, more even. "Sing anyway."

So I sang her a Trouble song—a sweet, slow song that Tyler had written just for me, for our wedding. I warbled off-key, but Jay didn't seem to mind. I sang until I thought she was asleep, her breathing deep. It was quiet, then, peaceful.

That's when she whispered, "He came to my room."

My heart lurched in my chest, my breath caught. "Who, Jay?"

"My stepfather." She didn't open her eyes, but her eyelids fluttered, and I saw a pained look cross her face.

I swallowed. "Did he touch you?"

"No." She swallowed, too, pulling the covers up to her chin, as if she couldn't get warm enough. "But he would have. He was going to. I couldn't stay anymore. I couldn't let him."

"Okay." I put my arm around her, feeling the slight tremble in her limbs. I'd suspected as much, even though when I'd asked in the past, Jay had skirted around the subject. "It's okay. You're okay now."

"I'm sorry," she said again, barely audible. Now that she'd confessed, her body relaxed. She started drifting off to sleep.

I couldn't help my own tears. I tucked her in and kissed her forehead, turning off the light before slipping out of her room.

Tyler was sitting up in bed when I came back to our room. He looked up and apologized before I could even open my mouth to tell him what she'd said.

"That bastard," Tyler said hoarsely, wrapping me in his arms and kissing my tears. "We can't send her back there."

"I know." I nodded against his chest.

I had no idea what to do.

I just knew I wanted to help her, any way I could.

Chapter Seven

I woke up briefly when Tyler got up at some ungodly hour to shower. He had the read-through today, he reminded me when I protested his getting out of bed. I woke up again when he kissed me goodbye, whispering that he'd see me for dinner.

"What am I cooking with my girls tonight?" he asked when I snaked my arms around his neck and tried to tempt him back to bed.

"Filet mignon," I murmured. "Asparagus and baby red potatoes."

"Sounds almost as delicious as you." He nuzzled my neck, smelling clean and fresh from the shower. "Listen. I'm gonna call Rob and straighten this whole thing out today, okay?"

"Should I call Sabrina, then?" I winced at the thought. If she really believed Jay had come on to Rob, I probably wouldn't get a word in edgewise during the lecture.

"No, just wait until after I talk to Rob." Tyler shook his head. "I'm also going to make an appointment with a lawyer."

"Divorcing me already?" I teased.

"Never." He nibbled at my collarbone and I let out a little sigh. "But we need to find out what sort of legal ground we stand on here, with Jay."

"You mean it?"

I'd been afraid, in the light of day, that he would reconsider the idea. Jay had shown up at our doorstep unannounced, at the worst possible time—the spotlight was on Trouble more than ever before now, and everything was tumultuous and upside down. I wouldn't have blamed him if he'd insisted on putting her on a plane back home the minute she stepped off. But he hadn't. Because he knew she was in trouble, and mostly, I think, because he was sweet and concerned, and he really wanted to help. And because he loved me, and would do anything for me.

"Of course I mean it." He pulled back to look at me in the early morning light. The sun was barely up. "I told you we'd work it out—and we will."

"My knight in shining armor." I kissed him, tasting toothpaste. "I love you, Ty."

"Love you, too, baby." He slowly withdrew, heading toward the door while I burrowed under the covers. "See you tonight."

Then he was gone.

I told myself—*ten more minutes*. Just ten more minutes and I'd get up, shower, and go wake sleepyhead Jay so we could get breakfast. She was a typical teen—she loved sleeping in. It was summer vacation, so I indulged her. Besides, I'd always been a big fan of sleeping in whenever possible, and when you were the wife of a rock star, late nights were common, so sleeping until noon started to become "the norm."

But Tyler's schedule had changed a lot, since he'd started shooting *Album*. Directors weren't just morning people—they liked everyone to be on-set at insanely early hours. It wasn't uncommon for Tyler to get up at three in the morning, to be on set by four or five. They had to do make-up before they were ready to shoot, but Tyler said he spent a lot of time in his trailer, waiting around.

He'd invited me to go with him, whenever I wanted—and I'd gone with him a few times. But me and five-in-the-morning didn't get along very well, and when I was overtired, I got extremely cranky, which just made for stupid arguments about nothing. That wasn't good for anyone. So Tyler said I should stay home and sleep. Sometimes I'd join him for lunch and hang around the set until dinner time, on shooting days. But today was just a read-through—they weren't filming the next season yet.

I should have set an alarm, but I didn't. Instead, I closed my eyes and drifted off and the next time I opened them, it was almost eleven. I checked the time on my phone, seeing Tyler had texted me at eight—*yawn* *miss you, love you*—and then there were Sabrina's calls from the night before that I hadn't returned.

I knew I was going to have to get Jay to tell me what, exactly, had happened with Rob. She'd said it was a mistake—a misunderstanding of some sort—and that Rob would confirm that. Maybe Tyler could just find out from Rob, I thought as I turned on the shower, and I wouldn't have to ask Jay at all. I didn't want a repeat of last night's tears and apologies. She'd been through enough.

I took a long, hot shower, thinking about calling Sabrina. She'd clearly overreacted, sending Jay home like that. Who had dropped her off? I wondered. Had she called Jesse and made him pick her up? Or had Rob taken her? No—it had to be Jesse. She wouldn't have let Rob be in a car alone with her.

Part of me understood Sabrina's anger and her slight paranoia. The last thing Trouble needed was a scandal, at this point. Things were already precarious, with Tyler leaving the band and things so up the air. They'd managed to recover from the scandal when Catherine had told the press their secrets, but it had been a long, hard road. For a long time, Catherine had played the victim, and Sabrina had been vilified as the fan-slut who had gotten pregnant and ended Rob's relationship with Catherine.

Then Catherine had gotten really desperate—shooting Sabrina had ultimately landed her in a mental hospital. I don't think it surprised anyone that Catherine committed suicide, after talking to the press and telling them about what had happened when they were just kids.

Except that it hadn't been a suicide, had it? Dante Marotta's reach had been long. He would have gone to any lengths to keep his secrets hidden, and that included putting an end to Catherine, who had dared to tell someone about them.

He would have ended all of us, I thought with a shiver, as I got dressed in jeans and a t-shirt. I'd told Jay we'd go swimming in the ocean today, but we could change into our suits later. If things had gone differently, we all would have ended up like Catherine.

But Dante was in jail, as were quite a few more high-profile people involved in the child prostitution ring he had been running. The scandal had been bad—but Rob and Tyler and Trouble had managed to keep their noses clean, and their deepest secrets—that Tyler had been the one who pulled the trigger, killing the man they'd all believed was their father—still secret.

I knew what Sabrina was worried about, having Jay around. If there was any hint of impropriety, the press would have a field day. It was what I'd been worried about, when I found Jay and her friends on the tour bus. The implications would be horrible, even if nothing had ever happened. It might be innocent until proven guilty in a court of law—but in the court of public opinion, it was more like "where there's smoke, there's fire." Thanks to Arnie's spin, Trouble had miraculously managed to keep their reputation, even if it had been slightly tarnished.

But the press had a long memory. Just the word "under age" would bring up old articles with phrases like "links to child prostitution." Trouble didn't need that sort of trouble, now or ever. That's what Tyler was worried about, that's what Rob and Sabrina were worried about, and I knew it was a real danger.

That scared me—but I also knew that Jay needed us. She needed our help. And entrusting her to a system like child welfare scared me even more. I'd heard Tyler's stories about living in foster care. I didn't want that for Jay.

One thing at a time, I told myself as I made my way down the hall to wake her up. First, breakfast. Then swimming. That was one thing about living near the ocean in California—almost every day was a good day for a swim. Then, tonight, we'd all make dinner together with Tyler. And we'd clear this thing up, with Rob and Sabrina.

Then, we'd talk to a lawyer, and hopefully he'd have a game plan.

Because we really needed a game plan.

"Jay?" I knocked on the door and waited. She didn't answer—not even a mumbled, *"go'wayit'stooearly!"* I knocked again. "Jay?"

I cocked my head, listening for the sound of running water. There was a bathroom off her bedroom, another reason I'd chosen it. A fifteen-year-old girl needed her own bathroom, given how much time they spent preening and pruning and strutting and selfie-ing. I'd never understood bathroom selfies—who wanted to take their picture with a toilet, sink and plunger as a backdrop?—but girls Jay's age took hundreds of them.

"Jay?" I opened her door, peeking in. I expected to see her dark head barely visible under the white-daisy comforter—I'd let her pick that out while we were at Macy's the day before, to replace the plain, "boring" navy-blue one that had been on the bed—just a snoring lump under the covers.

But she wasn't there.

And the bed wasn't just empty. It was made.

She'd been living with us a week, and she'd never once made her bed.

"Jay?" I called, louder this time, although part of me already knew it was a futile effort. "Jay, honey? Breakfast!"

As if I could tempt her with waffles and bacon.

I crossed her room and knocked on the bathroom door, but it swung open when I did. It was unlatched and dark. I flipped on the light, seeing all of her makeup, various bottles and tubes, were gone off the counter. I don't think I was even breathing when I opened her closet. All her new clothes were hung up, still there.

But the backpack she'd come with, that had been propped up on a chair in the corner, was gone.

"Jay," I whispered, sinking down onto the edge of the bed, my knees feeling like they wouldn't even hold me. "Where did you go?"

I didn't know the answer to that, but I knew she was gone. I could check the security log, but I was sure I'd find she'd bypassed our alarm—I'd told her the code just in case, along with the one to the main gate—and slipped away in the middle of the night.

She'd run away. Again.

I reached into my pocket, pulling out my phone. My first thought was to call the police—anyone who could help find her. But what could I say? If they ran her name in their system, would they find another missing person's report? Would they think we kidnapped her?

I opened my contacts and saw Jay's name. I held my breath and pushed "call." The phone rang once… twice… then I heard it. Opening the night stand drawer, I saw the pink case, my name on the display. She'd left the iPhone I'd bought her behind.

"Damnit," I swore, staring at my phone screen.

I'd have to call Tyler and tell him. We could decide what to do together.

I jumped when the doorbell rang, but my heart soared.

Jay!

It wasn't the main door—it was the bell that rang when someone was at the gate outside. It could have been anyone—Rob, Sabrina, the UPS guy—but I

- 111 -

prayed it was Jay, who had gone for a long walk to think, but had changed her mind about leaving and had come home.

I ran to our room—we had an intercom there—and pressed the button to talk.

"Hello?"

"Katie?" Leanne's voice came through and my heart sank. "It's just me. Sorry I didn't call, but—"

The last of her words were garbled.

"Come on in," I told her, pressing the button to open the gates.

I went downstairs to let her in, opening the door just as she was about to ring the bell.

"Oh, hi." Leanne smiled, then she saw my face, and her smile disappeared. "Katie, what's the matter?"

"It's Jay," I croaked, my voice sounding strained and full of tears.

"Your cousin?"

"She's not my cousin," I confessed, putting my face in my hands. "And she's run away!"

"Okay." Leanne took a deep breath, stepping into the house. "Come on. Let's go sit down and you can tell me everything."

We went to the kitchen, and I told her everything while I made coffee. I told her about finding Jay on Trouble's tour bus when she was just twelve—with her two older girlfriends and an eight-ball of heroin. I told her how I'd introduced Jay to Rob, so he could let her down easy and tell her that he was in love with and engaged to Sabrina, and would be marrying her as soon as his divorce with Catherine was final.

I poured us coffee and told her how I confiscated their drugs and put all three of the girls on a Greyhound bus back to home. I gave them all my cell phone number, in case they ran into a problem. Jay had been the only one to use it, letting me know when she was home safe. Her mother hadn't even missed her, she said.

That was the beginning, I told Leanne. We'd stayed in touch. Jay liked to turn to me when she was having problems at home or at school. She was an average student—but she got a lot of attention from boys. Especially older boys. I'd done my best, I told Leanne, giving her long-distance advice, trying to be both a friend and an adult, trying to steer her in the right direction.

I told Leanne about Jay's alcoholic father and neglectful mother, how her father had left—*yay!*—and then her mother had found a replacement that was actually far worse—*boo!* And then, how Jay had run away, coming to us for help, and we'd taken her in

"So why would she run away from you?" Leanne asked, putting cream in her coffee, and so I told her that, too. What had happened last night, how Sabrina had sent her home because of some misunderstanding between Jay and Rob—no, I didn't know the specifics, not yet—and how Jay had sobbed and apologized and told me it was all a mistake.

"Well, you can understand Sabrina's reaction," Leanne mused.

I said I could—of course, I could. They'd had issues before, with fans who wanted a job just to get

- 113 -

close to Rob. Nannies, in fact. I didn't blame her. But it had been devastating to Jay.

"Then, Tyler went off on her." I winced at the memory. "He said he wanted her to send her home. I think that's what did it. I think Jay ran away before we could send her back..."

"Well, her mother must be looking for her," Leanne said. "Maybe that would be the best thing?"

"Not if her stepfather's in the house," I snapped. "She says he hasn't done anything... yet. But he will. If we give him the opportunity, he will."

"Well, if she's in danger... maybe you should just let the police and the system handle it?" Leanne suggested, shrugging when I glared at the idea. "It might be safer for everyone."

"Everyone but Jay." I shook my head vehemently. "They won't take her away until something happens. We both know that."

"Call Tyler," she suggested. "He's got access to resources. Maybe you can find her before she gets too far."

I nodded, reaching for my phone, hoping to see a message from Jay, maybe made from a pay phone, but there was nothing. I called Tyler, but it went straight to voicemail. The read-through, of course. He would have muted it.

"Ty, it's me," I said, leaving a message, watching Leanne put a rectangular box on the table. She'd been carrying it under her arm when she came in, but I hadn't really acknowledged it—I'd been too worried about Jay. "Listen, as soon as you get this, I need you to call me. Jay... I can't find her. Her backpack is gone. I think she's run away from us. I

- 114 -

think... please, just call me. As soon as you get this. Please."

I hung up, staring at the phone in my hand.

"Look at this." Leanne pulled a photograph out of the box, handing it over to me.

"Awww." Jeez, my ovaries were sensitive to babies. My biological clock was ticking away like a time bomb down there. "Wait... is this... is that Tyler?"

"Yes." Leanne's smile was filled with both sadness and a sort of motherly pride. "Wasn't he darling?"

"Look at all that blonde hair." The little boy in the photograph couldn't have been more than a year old—he was standing holding onto a coffee table, balancing between it and a dirty, flower-colored sofa, wearing only a drooping diaper. His smile lit up his whole face. I would have recognized it anywhere. Tyler. My Tyler.

"Are there more?" I looked at the box, holding out greedy hands for it.

"Lots," Leanne agreed, pushing the box over to me. She was holding a photograph in her hand. "You can go through them all later. After we find Jay."

I nodded, glancing into the box that held all that was left of Tyler and Rob and Sarah's history with their mother. It broke my heart.

"But I wanted to show you this. Actually, I wanted to show it to Tyler... I wasn't sure what to do with it. About it... I guess..." The scar on Leanne's face seemed to droop at her words, and her one good eye flitted from the photograph in her hand up to me and back again. "Here. You tell me."

- 115 -

"Is this Sarah?" I asked, smiling at the dark-haired girl in the picture. She looked to be about kindergarten age, wearing a short summer dress, holding one of those orange sherbet Push-Up ice creams. She was in mid-lick, the ice cream dripping down toward her elbow, her head tilted sideways, half-smiling for whoever was holding the camera.

"Yes." Leanne nodded, pursing her lips. "At my mother's place. That was after... after they were taken away. After Tyler... after Joe was killed. I was in jail."

"I thought they were separated?" I frowned, staring at the picture. "Weren't they all put into foster care?"

"My mother had the kids for a month or so, before that," she explained. "They might've given her custody, if it wasn't for the fire."

"The fire?"

"She fell asleep," Leanne said. "Passed out, more like."

"And there was a fire?"

"Smokers shouldn't drink." She pointed to the photograph. "This must have been taken then. Do you see who's standing in the background?"

"Is that... Dante?" I'd only seen Tyler's real father once in person—although as California state prosecutor, I'd seen pictures of him in the paper. He was in a lot of them after his arrest.

Leanne nodded. "Do you recognize anyone else?"

I squinted at the men standing in the background. They were slightly out of focus, standing in a group on the driveway, four of them. Dante was tall and recognizable—he was even looking over at Sarah, a fact I found ominous, now that I knew what sort of operation he was running, and continued to run. Two men had their backs to the camera, so Leanne could only be talking about the other man standing beside Dante.

"I don't—" I shook my head, looking at the man beside Dante. He was much shorter and he was sporting a goatee and pornstache, probably to make up for the way his hair was thinning on top.

"He's younger." Leanne's voice was soft, but she sounded sure of herself. "More hair. The beard probably throws it off. But it's him."

"Arnie." I stared at the photograph in my hand, watching it tremble. What did this mean? Arnie and Dante? Long, long before Arnie had "discovered" Rob, helping him find Tyler and Sarah while he put the rest of Trouble together.

"It's him." Leanne's one good eye looked at me, unblinking.

"How?" I shook my head, confused. "Did he know Dante?"

"I don't know." She sat back with a long sigh. "But... I had a bad feeling about him, when we were at Rob's. Last week? Remember?"

I remembered—when Tyler had made his announcement.

"Bad feeling?" I looked more closely at the photograph. The more I looked at it, the more I was sure—it was Arnie. He was younger, thinner, and he had more hair—but there was no doubt, it was him. "What do you mean?"

- 117 -

"I... let's just say, I didn't like the way he looked at Jay," she said. "That whole modeling thing? It just... felt wrong."

"You think..." I didn't want to say it out loud. The thought made my whole body break out in goose flesh.

"I didn't want to say anything." Leanne sipped her coffee, looking at me over the rim. "I thought I was just jumping to conclusions. But then I saw that photograph... and I knew I had to tell someone."

"I have to call Tyler." I pulled my phone back out, hitting redial.

Answer, answer, answer, I thought, closing my eyes and willing him to pick up. I needed him to pick up.

"This is Ty, leave me a message."

Beep.

Goddamnit. I hung up, not leaving a message, and looking through my contacts for the studio number. I could get one of the girls at the front desk to go get him.

"No luck?" Leanne asked as the studio phone started ringing.

Lindsay answered—I recognized her voice, and she knew me, thankfully, so when I asked her to go get Tyler, she didn't think it was weird.

"Oh, hey, Katie," she said, and I heard phones ringing in the background. She wasn't the only one manning the desk up front. "I think they're done for the day. Ended about an hour ago?"

"Really?" I frowned. "He said he wouldn't be home until dinner..."

"I don't know," Lindsay said, not sounding concerned. "Maybe he had another meeting? I saw that reporter from Variety skulking around earlier."

I stiffened, my lips barely forming the words. "Alisha McKenna?"

"Uh-huh," Lindsay agreed. "If he comes back in, I'll have him call you."

"Okay, thanks." I ended the call, glaring at my phone.

Alisha McKenna. Alisha-*fuck-me*-McKenna.

"Everything okay?" Leanne asked as I searched my apps for *"Find iPhone."* Our accounts were connected, and I could track Tyler anytime, anywhere. I'd told him that when we'd signed the contract for our phones, and he'd kissed me and said, "I love it when your eyes get green like that."

"Yeah, I just—" My voice trailed off as the little dot blinked on the map, showing me where Tyler was right that moment. "Oh my God."

"What?"

"He's downtown—L.A."

"So?" She cocked her head at me but I barely registered it.

"At the Hilton. *He's at a hotel.*"

"Katie!" she called after me, but I already had my keys in my hand and I was heading toward the door.

"I'll drive." That's all Leanne said, and I let her.

I was shaking too much to try operating a motorized vehicle, anyway.

I had no idea what I was going to do, when we got to the hotel. I had visions of knocking on every single door at the Hilton, looking for my husband. Because of course they wouldn't tell me where he was. I could imagine the smirk on the clerk's face when I asked if Tyler Cook had checked in—or Warren Peace. That was the ridiculous "punny" pseudonym he liked to use.

But he wouldn't use Warren, would he?

Not if he didn't want me to find him.

The thought of Tyler checking into a hotel in the middle of the afternoon with *her*—Alisha-*I'll-Do-Anything-For-An-Interview-including-you*-McKenna—made my whole body shake with anger.

"Katie, breathe," Leanne murmured, patting the hand resting on my knee. "I'm sure it's not what you're thinking."

"It better not be," I said darkly, trying to wish the traffic away.

On my phone, the blue dot was still there, blinking inside the L.A. Hilton. A hotel in the middle of the afternoon. What else could it be?

It was bad enough that Jay had gone missing—and I had no idea what to do about that. It was worse that Leanne had found that strange, incriminating photo of Arnie from a million years ago. I didn't like any of the things it might imply, and I really didn't like Leanne's "bad feeling" about the whole thing.

But the fact that my husband wasn't answering his phone and I'd found him at the Hilton was just the cherry on the cake of my already crappy day. I'd dismembered him every which way in my head by the time Leanne pulled up to the front and handed the keys to the Subaru Tyler had bought for her to the valet.

"Katie, wait for me," she called, huffing as she tried to keep up.

I looked at my phone, swearing at the GPS map. It showed Tyler's phone, and now mine, close together. But it wasn't clear enough for me to tell just exactly where he was. Which room?

"Katie." Leanne's hand on my arm. I looked up at her, then followed the line of her finger, where she was pointing.

It was Tyler, sitting in the restaurant. He was facing us, although he hadn't seen me or his mother. He nodded and said something to the person across from him. I couldn't see who it was, because they were in a booth.

Lunch. He'd just gone to lunch. Probably with a co-star or maybe he'd called Rob to meet him. I was so stupid, doubting him, even for a second, and I felt instantly ashamed. My cheeks flushed with it.

I stood, frozen, unsure whether to go forward or turn around and go home. But I had to talk to him. Jay was gone—and then there was the picture Leanne had stuck in her purse.

"It's okay," I breathed, looking at Leanne, seeing the concern on her face. I started across the lobby, heading for Tyler, so relieved my knees almost buckled with it. "I just—"

Then I stopped.

Tyler was sitting across from a woman.

Which, in and of itself, wasn't a big deal.

But the woman was a redhead—no doubt about that. She was leaning over in the booth, maybe rummaging in her purse, so I couldn't see her face— her long red hair fell across her cheek.

- 121 -

But I saw her name flash in my head, like a neon sign.

Alisha McKenna.

"Sonofabitch," I whispered.

"Katie," Leanne warned, grabbing my arm, but it was too late.

I'd already decided.

I was going to kill her.

With my bare hands.

Chapter Eight

"You can't," Tyler said, leaning back in the booth. I was close enough now to see there was no food in front of either of them. "Those records are sealed."

"Leaks happen," the redhead said with a shrug.

Tyler looked up as I approached and I saw his eyes light up in surprise—*yeah I bet you're surprised, Mr. Hotel in the Afternoon*—but I was focused on the ginger in front of him. I'd deal with Tyler after I shaved her head, dipped her in honey and set her on an ant hill. Or something equally awful.

"What in the hell do you think you're doing?" I snapped. Leanne came up behind me, and I heard Tyler say, "Mom?" but I ignored that too.

"Excuse me?" The redhead looked up at me, and I saw instantly that she wasn't *the* redhead. Alisha McKenna had freckles, and while her hair was the same color, I realized, now that I was up close, that the clothes were all wrong. This woman was wearing a respectable pant suit Hillary Clinton would be envious of. Alisha liked skirts and low-cut blouses. Alisha reminded me of a ginger Jennifer Tilly. This woman was more Julianne Moore.

"Katie." Tyler stood, taking my arm, frowning at me, then at his mother, like he wasn't sure what in the hell we were doing here, but he didn't like it. "Uh... excuse us for a moment..."

He moved to lead me away, but I wasn't having it.

"I'm not going anywhere." I shook Tyler's hand off my arm. "Until you tell me what Ms. Silence of the Lambs is doing here."

Tyler looked at me, stunned. Then he looked at the redhead and burst out laughing.

"Goddamnit, Tyler," I hissed, punching his shoulder, which caused patrons in the restaurant to turn to look at us. "What in the hell is going on?"

"Sit down, Mrs. Cook," the redhead nodded at the booth seat opposite her. "I can explain."

"Can you?" I snapped, letting Tyler push me into the booth. "You'd better!"

"This is my mother," Tyler told the redhead. "Leanne—"

"I know who she is." The redhead slid closer to the wall, making room for Leanne, who slid in, looking wary.

"You do?" I looked from Tyler to the redhead to Leanne, confused. "Who in the hell are you?"

"Agent Wendy Fuller." The redhead's voice was low and she glanced around before reaching inside her jacket and flashing her identification. I saw Leanne's face turn stark white. My stomach dropped to my toes.

"FBI?" I whispered.

"You were spot-on," Tyler said with a chuckle, putting an arm around my shoulder. "That Silence of the Lambs thing. Funny."

"I'm not laughing." I sat back, stunned, then looked up at Tyler. "What is this about? What in the hell is going on? Is this about Jay? Oh God…"

"Jay?" Wendy asked.

- 124 -

"Jessica Finlay." Tyler nodded at Wendy, and I felt him stiffen beside me. "Show her."

"Show me what?"

But Wendy the FBI agent was already going into the briefcase beside her. I expected something—I don't know what, papers or photographs or something—but she pulled out an iPad and typed on the screen.

"What about Jay?" I asked, feeling panicked. "This is about Jay? Is she okay? What—?"

"She's with Arnie." Leanne's voice was soft, but she spoke the truth. Wendy turned the iPad toward me, and I saw pictures of Jay—going into Arnie's office. Coming out of his office, his arm around her shoulder. "He took it over, didn't he?"

"It? What?" I asked, but Wendy was already telling us.

The pictures were recent—taken just that morning.

Of course, that's where Jay had gone. She'd had Arnie's card, and he was the only other person in the whole city she knew, besides us. He'd offered to help her, hadn't he? Said he could get her a modeling job…

"I have something to show you," Leanne said, after Wendy had told us that they'd had Arnie under surveillance since they'd arrested Dante. They'd suspected he was involved, but they hadn't been able to gather enough evidence to arrest him.

"He has Jay." I grabbed Tyler's arm and he squeezed me tighter. "Oh God, he has Jay…"

"He's not stupid." Wendy held her hand out as Leanne passed the old photograph across the table.

"He wouldn't groom someone so close to you. He thinks she's your cousin—that's what Tyler said. If he was offering her a modeling job, it would likely be something legitimate."

"Unless he finds out she isn't your cousin.," Leanne said, watching Wendy's face as she squinted at the photograph. Her words made me sick to my stomach.

"What is that?" Tyler asked, as Wendy handed the photograph of a younger, skinnier Arnie across the table so he could see it. "Is that... holy fuck."

"You didn't believe her, did you?" Leanne asked her son, seeing the shock on his face.

"I didn't know what to believe." Tyler stared at the picture in his hand. "FBI shows up and wants to talk to me, what am I supposed to say? I said I'd have lunch. So here we are."

"Did you know he was involved?" Wendy asked, glancing over at Leanne.

"No. I didn't know him back then." Leanne shook her head. "And I didn't have this picture until last week."

"This could be very useful." Wendy took the picture from Tyler, looking at it again. I could practically see the wheels turning.

I had barely recovered from the fact that she wasn't Alisha McKenna—but I suddenly had the feeling that this woman was far more dangerous, and wielded much more power.

"Look, I told you," Tyler said, talking to Wendy, but keeping his voice down. "I don't care what you're holding over my head. I'm not getting in the middle of this."

"Holding over your head?" My eyes narrowed at the agent. "What are you holding over his head?"

"She threatened to leak the truth to the press," Leanne said softly. "That's it, isn't it? That Tyler was the one who really pulled the trigger?"

"I don't care." Tyler shook his head. "Leak away."

"Okay, listen." Wendy sighed, putting the old photograph on the table. "This is proof, right here, that Arnold was involved, even back then."

"Well…" Tyler hesitated, frowning at the picture. "I don't know."

"What more do you need?" the redheaded agent asked, her brow knitting with frustration. "I can understand having some loyalty—but doesn't this show you that this man was clearly involved? He was involved then—and he's involved now. These are children we're talking about. Children like Jessica Finlay."

Wendy touched the iPad she'd put on the table, waking the screen up, where Jay was being led out of Arnie's office, his arm around her shoulder. I made a little noise in my throat when I saw it, looking up at Tyler.

"What does she want you to do?" I asked.

"Wear a wire." Wendy zoomed in on the iPad screen, on Jay's face. She looked both hopeful and scared. It broke my heart. "We need a confession."

"He won't tell me, anyway." Tyler squeezed my shoulder, looking over at Wendy. "I get why you came to me—I'm the only one you've got leverage over. But I don't think he'd say anything, even if I walked in there with this picture. Why would he?"

"Tyler's right." Leanne spoke up. "He could come up with a million reasons why he was there that day. Trouble is his meal ticket. He wouldn't jeopardize that."

"I can try," Tyler offered, frowning. "If he really is... what you say he is. I can try. But I think I might do more harm than good."

"You may be right." Wendy tapped her finger on the old photograph thoughtfully.

"I'm sorry," Tyler apologized.

"He'll tell me." Leanne's words were so soft I almost didn't hear her.

"Mom." Tyler's voice had a warning in it. "No."

"Think about it." She looked across the table at her son with her one good eye. Beside her, Wendy was listening very carefully. "If I take this picture to him—if I threaten him with exposure. If I tell him I know he's involved, and I ask him for money—a little blackmail in exchange for my silence? That would be enough, wouldn't it, to put him away?"

"No," Tyler growled, his arm tightening around my shoulder. "I won't allow it. It's too dangerous."

"It could work." Wendy chewed on her lower lip, then she turned to Leanne. "You'd be willing to wear a wire?"

"Yes." Tyler's mother ignored his protest. "I'll do it."

"Let me make a call..." Wendy got out of the booth—Leanne moved so she could climb out—while Tyler went off on his mother.

"You are not doing this!" he snapped as Leanne slid back into the booth while Wendy walked away, already on her phone. "Do you hear me?"

"Tyler, stop." Leanne picked up the photograph of Sarah, half-smiling at the camera, licking her ice cream, and her one good eye filled with tears. "I was a horrible mother. I know that. I was an addict, and I sacrificed everything for that addiction. Even my children."

"Mom." Tyler's voice was hoarse. "Don't."

"It's the least I can do." She lifted her ravaged face to his, the unblemished, still-pretty side wet with tears. "Your uncle's dead, and your father's in jail, and yet it's still happening. They're still hurting kids."

"Jay," I said softly. The thought of her with Arnie—Arnie, who we trusted, who had always said he was looking out for us—made me sick.

"Yes, like Jay." Leanne leaned in to take Tyler's hand, which was balled into a fist on the table. "Tyler, I want to do this. I saw the way he looked at her. He's dangerous. He's very, very dangerous."

"I can't fucking believe this." Tyler looked down at his mother's hands, cupped over his fist. "He did this? He really did this?"

"He's been doing it for years." Leanne used one hand to swipe at the tears on her cheek. "I think that's how he knew how to find you. He and Dante knew all along. They kept tabs on all three of you. They *used* you."

"You guys were quite a meal ticket," I whispered, the realization sinking in like a lead weight in my belly. "He created Trouble, Ty. Isn't that what you told me? He put the band together..."

"I'll kill him," Tyler snarled, and I grabbed onto him to keep him from getting up and taking off.

"No!" I cried, and Leanne did too, at the same time.

"Let me do this," Tyler's mother pleaded. "He'll tell me—and he'll go to jail. Just like your father."

"I'd rather kill him," he spat, but he stayed in his seat as Wendy approached.

"It's a go." She stood beside the table, looking at the three of us. "If you're still willing?"

"Yes," Leanne assured her.

"No!" Tyler cried.

"We'll make sure she's safe," the agent assured him. "I promise you."

"Mom." Tyler was the one pleading now. "It's too dangerous. Don't do this. You can't do this."

"I can." Leanne stood, giving him a sad, twisted smile. "And I will. For you and Robbie and Sarah. And for little Jay. And my grandchildren. I am going to do this."

"Come with me." Wendy grabbed her briefcase, shoving the iPad and photograph inside, before taking Leanne's arm and starting leading her away.

"Ty." I whispered his name, grabbing on to him when he went to bolt. "No... let her go. Let her... please..."

"Katie, I can't," he choked, and I put my arms around him, holding him close. "What if something happens to her?"

"She wants to do this. For you. Let her be your mother."

I watched Leanne following the agent, and I knew exactly what she was feeling. I wasn't a mother—I didn't know if I ever would be one, given how Tyler felt about having kids—but since Jay had come to us, I knew how it felt to be protective, to feel like you'd do anything, even sacrifice yourself, to save a child.

"I have to tell Rob." Tyler put his arms around me for a moment, breathing deep, trying to stay calm, I knew.

"It's okay," I told him. "I'll come with you. I'm here, baby. I'm here."

"Thank God." He held me so close for a moment I thought he'd break my ribs.

It happened fast, but it felt so slow.

Rob and Sabrina didn't believe us, not at first. Tyler had to call Wendy, who texted him a copy of Leanne's photograph. There was sweet little Sarah and her ice cream—with her father, Dante, in the background, and the man who had created Trouble standing right beside him.

"Arnie." Rob would have thrown Tyler's phone if Sabrina hadn't grabbed it. "I'm going to kill him!"

"That's what I said." Tyler snarled at the photograph when Sabrina gave him back his phone.

When we told them what Leanne was going to do—the she was going to put on a wire and confront Arnie, to get him to confess, and perhaps implicate others—they didn't believe that, either. At least, Rob didn't. Not until Wendy showed up at their house, except this time she wasn't alone. Her partner was a tall, dark-haired guy with angular features who said his name was Jordan and they both flashed their I.D.

"Did you find Jay?" was the first thing I asked. "Can you bring her here?"

"Jessica Finlay," Wendy told her partner, Jordan.

"We're working on it, ma'am," he assured me.

Working on it. Great.

"But where is she?" I asked. "Is she with him?"

"She's safe," Wendy said. "We'll bring her here as soon as we can."

"Is she with the FBI?" I couldn't let it go.

"We've got some questions for you," Jordan interrupted me. "For all of you. Where's Sarah?"

We hadn't told Sarah yet.

Sabrina called her, and she came with Anne. By then, Celeste and Jesse had been informed, and Daisy had started doing what she did whenever anything happy or sad happened—she made us all food.

They wanted to talk to Rob, Tyler and Sarah alone, so I went upstairs to help Sabrina get Lucy and Henry up from their nap.

"I'm sorry, Katie," Sabrina said, lifting Henry from his crib. Lucy was already calling for me, so I went to get her. "I should have listened to Rob—he kept telling me I was overreacting. I shouldn't have sent her home."

"It's okay." I kissed Lucy's cheek and she put her arms around my neck. "I don't blame you."

I didn't ask her what had happened, what Jay had done. Whatever it was, Rob knew Jay hadn't meant to do anything wrong. That's what mattered.

Now all I could think about was getting Jay back, safe and sound. After that, we'd deal with whatever came. One thing at a time.

We stayed in the nursery for a while, letting the kids crawl and toddle around, until Daisy called on the intercom to say she had food ready.

Downstairs in the kitchen, Tyler and Rob were talking at the table. Sarah hugged me as we came in, and ended up taking Lucy from my arms. Tyler held out a hand to me and I went to sit beside him. Daisy put food on the table, but I couldn't even look at it. The smell of it made me nauseous.

"What's happening?" I asked Tyler softly.

"Come on." He took my hand and led me out of the kitchen. We went out the glass patio door, where it was a perfect California day. The sun was still shining, reflecting off the pool out back.

Tyler sat in one of the patio chairs, under an umbrella, and I sat beside him. He took my hand, squeezing it.

"It's going to be okay," he told me. "Whatever happens, we're going to be okay."

"I'm not so sure about that." I watched the water, the little points of sunlight almost blinding. "I heard what Wendy said about the guys."

"You did?" His eyebrows went up. "Sneak."

I shrugged. It wasn't on purpose. I'd been on my way downstairs for a sippy cup for Henry. Wendy and Jordan had been meeting with Rob, Tyler and Sarah in the living room. That's when I'd overheard Wendy saying that they suspected that at least two of Trouble's other band members were involved, and knew what Arnie was doing.

"But they don't suspect you or Rob?" I asked, glancing toward the house. "Right?"

"No." His thumb moved over my wedding ring, shifting it back and forth. "They know we're not involved."

"Trouble." I shook my head, trying to absorb it. "It's…"

"Over." Tyler let out a sigh.

"I'm so sorry, Ty." I squinted up at the sky, trying to judge how much time had passed. It seemed to have stopped, while we could do nothing but sit here and wait.

"I was already out," he reminded me. "Rob… it's killing him."

"Yeah." I gave a little shiver. "He finds out both his agent and probably two, if not all three, of the guys left in his band are involved in a child prostitution ring. I'd say that's a pretty bad day."

"I just wanted you to know that Jay's okay."

"What?" I sat up, looking at him. "How do you know?"

"Arnie had her put up in an apartment in L.A." His mouth tightened for a moment, then he said. "I guess he keeps them there, at first. While he's…"

"Grooming them," I finished, my hand tightening in his. "Jesus, Ty. He really is…"

"Yeah." He gritted his teeth and closed his eyes for a minute. "Listen, they checked to see if Jay's mom had called the cops. There's no missing person's report. Nothing's been filed."

I gaped at him. "Nothing? At all?"

"No." He sighed. "Which is actually good news, for us. We still have to talk to a lawyer, but I think we have a good shot. Better than I thought."

"A good shot…" I swallowed, trying to catch my breath. "At… what? Exactly."

He looked at me, puzzled. "Well, keeping her. What else?"

"Oh Ty." I threw myself at him, and the tears I'd been holding in since I found Jay gone finally came in a huge rush of emotion.

"Shhh." He soothed, rocking me in his lap. "Hey, come on, what's this? I thought you'd be happy?"

"I am happy," I choked. I'd been so afraid for Jay—afraid we'd lost her, afraid we wouldn't be able to help her, that we wouldn't be able to save her. The thought that we really might be able to keep her, as ours, I'd shoved so far back in my mind, I'd barely dared to hope.

"You mean it?" I asked him in a near whisper. "She's a handful, you know. I mean, taking on a teenager... you're really up for that? I know she sort of came out of nowhere, and we didn't have time to think or talk about it, let alone plan, but..."

"Katie." He pressed his finger to my lips, giving a little shake of his head. "Stop. You love her. I love you. That's all."

I put my arms around him and kissed him, tears and all. Tyler kissed me back, holding me tight, tighter. I let out a little gasp and he let me go, meeting my eyes.

"Hey." He smiled, cupping my face in his hands, wiping my wet cheeks with his thumbs. "You think Jay will be okay with a little brother or sister?"

"Yeah, right." I gave a little laugh, but Tyler didn't laugh with me. I blinked at him, trying to find my voice. "You're... you're kidding. Aren't you?"

"No." His gaze searched my face. "Don't you want to?"

"Wait a minute." I shook my head, as if to clear it. "You're serious? You're talking about having kids? Like, yours and mine? Sperm and egg? A little Tyler junior?"

"Yeah." He nodded. "Unless... you don't want to...?"

"Are you kidding me?" I half-laughed, pressing my forehead to his, closing my eyes. "My uterus has had a vacancy sign on it since I met you."

"Well, okay then." He chuckled. Then he sobered up. "You know, I used to be scared that if I had a kid... it would get this damned family curse..."

"You're not cursed." I took his hand, kissing the back of his knuckles.

"Sometimes it feels like we are." He sighed. "Just when I think things are looking up... I feel like the wizard."

"The wizard?"

"Of Oz." He laughed at the puzzled look on my face. "It's one of the movies I remember watching with my mom, when I was little."

The thought of Leanne made me feel cold and I snuggled closer to him. I didn't like to think what she was facing, with Arnie, right this very moment.

"The wizard?" I asked again.

"Yeah. Remember that hot air balloon he had?" I nodded. "Uh-huh."

"I feel like I'm always trying to get it off the ground, you know? And just when I do... just when it starts sailing through the air... wham! Something happens and I'm falling again..."

"It's not a hot air balloon." I tucked my head under his chin. "It's a roller coaster."

"Life?"

I nodded. "Our life. It's a roller coaster. Up and down. Up and down. Curves here, curves there. Sometimes you see them coming—sometimes you don't."

"Huh." His arms tightened around me. "Yeah… I guess it is more like a roller coaster."

"Make sure we're buckled in," I said with a smile. "Then we can hang on and enjoy the ride."

That made him laugh and he kissed my cheek. "I wouldn't want to take this ride with anyone else."

"Me either," I agreed, clinging to him.

The glass patio door opened behind us and I glanced over, expecting Daisy to be there, asking if we wanted anything to eat. But it wasn't Daisy.

It was Jay.

"Ty," I whispered, shaking him so he would look, and he did, just as I scrambled off his lap.

"Jay!" I cried, and then she was running to me, putting her arms around me, sobbing and apologizing, all of nearly unintelligible.

"I didn't know where else to go," she gasped as we hugged and rocked on our feet. "I'm sorry, I'm so sorry!"

"I'm just glad you're safe," I told her. "We're just glad you're home safe."

"We are." Tyler was there, too, putting his arms around us both. "You're safe, Jay. You'll be safe with us, I promise you."

His words made me cry, so then both me and Jay were crying and apologizing for crying, and then were laughing because of all the apologizing, and that's when the back door opened again.

"Hey." Rob called out to his brother. "They arrested him. Nick and Jon, too."

"Not Kenny?" I asked, stunned by the news.

"No." Rob shook his head, looking as incredulous as I felt. It was like we'd all been run over by a freight train today. "Kenny didn't know anything about it. But Arnie implicated both Nick and Jon."

"Where's Mom?" Tyler asked, taking my hand and pulling me toward the house. Jay wouldn't let go of my other hand, so she followed. "Is she all right?"

"She's fine," Wendy called from somewhere inside. I glanced in and saw her on the phone. "They're bringing her here."

"Thank God." I breathed, and I felt Tyler relax, too.

Inside, everyone was talking at once. The news had come in—that Jay was safe, that Arnie'd been arrested—and the relief in the room was palpable. Jay took some cookies off a tray, sharing some with Lucy, and Sabrina smiled as she watched them. So that was over, too—thank goodness. Whatever ill-will that had formed there had dissipated.

When Leanne appeared in the doorway of the kitchen, I thought it would be Tyler or Sarah who went to her. But it wasn't. The first person who went to her was Rob. He put his arms around her, giving her a long, hard hug. I don't know what he said to her—his words were clearly only meant for her—but whatever he said caused long streaks of tears down the side of her face as she hugged him back.

I watched Tyler and Sarah hug their mother, too, feeling slightly misty, but it wasn't until Jay walked

- 138 -

over with Lucy in her arms and handed the little dark-haired girl to her grandmother that the waterworks really started.

"Here." Celeste handed me a box of Kleenex and I took one, wiping the tears falling down my cheeks.

"This is crazy," I gasped, laughing through my tears at the insanity of it all.

Trouble was dead, with two band members going to jail along with Arnie. But there was Leanne, finally fully reunited with her family, including her last, angry son and her two beautiful grandbabies. And Jay, who was smiling and happy and, hopefully, ours. And Tyler had a part in a new movie, along with the series.

We'd probably be making a baby in New Zealand this year.

How could I feel so sad and so happy all at the same time?

"This is life." Tyler put an arm around my shoulder, leaning in to kiss my wet cheek. "You were right. It's a goddamned roller coaster ride. Buckle up, baby."

I laughed and put my arms around him, holding on tight. "As long as we're in it together."

Epilogue

"Mom!"

I sighed and Tyler laughed, wrapping me in a hug as I headed toward our bedroom door.

"You wanted to be Mom," he reminded me, nuzzling my ear and pinning me against a nearby wall.

"You better quit, or you're gonna make me 'Mom' again," I teased, sliding my thigh between his.

"Tempting." His hands were already edging my skirt up.

"Mom!" Jay called again from her room down the hall. "Help!"

"Coming!" I called, straightening my skirt before knocking on her door. "Jay?"

"I'm stuck," she called. "Open the door!"

I did, laughing when I saw her half-in and half-out of her graduation gown.

"My hair's stuck," she complained from underneath. "In the zipper."

I helped her get unstuck, putting her gown on the bed, along with her cap, while Jay wiggled into her the dress she'd picked for her graduation party.

"Did you see the card?" I asked, biting my lip as I sat on the edge of her bed. "Dad said he left it for you."

"Yeah." Jay sat in front of her vanity, reapplying her make-up. "I called her. She said congrats."

"We would have flown her out…"

"She didn't want to come." Jay shrugged. "It's okay, Mom. I'm okay."

"Yes, you are." I went over to her, putting my arms around her neck and kissing the top of her head. "I'm so proud of you. We couldn't be prouder."

"Thanks." Her smile was bright and beautiful, just like she was.

I couldn't believe it had been three years already. Jay had spent the first half of her sophomore year with a tutor while we filmed in New Zealand and the lawyers hammered out agreements.

Jay's mother hadn't put up much of a fight— which was awful for Jay, on the one hand, but great for her, on the other. Because she was happy with us, and we couldn't have been happier having her.

When we'd come home, she asked if she could go to school, so we'd found a private one, something co-ed, per her request. Although to my surprise, boys hadn't been that much of an issue. She'd dated a few, but she hadn't settled on any one guy.

She'd found a love for reading—and writing. And she was quite good. We'd spent months researching and sending college applications, and she'd been accepted to almost all of them. I'd been afraid she'd go to the east coast, to one of the more prestigious schools she'd applied to—"I just wanted to see if I could get in," she said later—but she decided on UCLA. Some place closer to home.

"Jayyyyy!" Lucy's footsteps came pounding up the stairs.

"Coming!" Jay called, laughing and twirling in her dress. "What do you think? Good enough?"

"You're beautiful," I told her, and then Lucy was bursting in, hugging Jay around the waist.

"I guess this means your mom and dad are here?" I asked Lucy, getting up off the bed.

"Yup." Lucy nodded, giving me a gap-toothed smile. She was in kindergarten this year and growing like a weed. She looked more like Sabrina every day. "But Henry's home. He's got a rash. Mom says it might be chicken pox."

"Oh great," I said, heading toward the door. "Let's hope you're not all contagious."

"Did I hear Lucy?" Tyler looked up at me when I opened our bedroom door. He was sitting on the bed, barefoot, a guitar in his lap, strumming idly.

"Rob and Sabrina are here. I can smell Daisy's food." I sniffed the air, smiling. "I'm so glad Sabrina let me borrow her today."

"Guess we better head downstairs before everyone else arrives." Ty smiled at me, changing chords. "Hm. I'm a little rusty."

"You'll do fine." I leaned over his guitar and kissed him. "Jay will love it—you and Rob and Sabrina playing for her graduation."

"Just a few songs," he reminded me with a little snort. "We all know everyone wants to see the big stars."

"Ha." I wrinkled my nose at him. "You're a bigger star than both of them, these days. Mr. Oscar-winner."

"Double platinum," he countered, setting his acoustic aside. "Sold out in every single city on tour."

- 142 -

"Katie!" I heard Sabrina calling up the stairs. "Daisy can't find the food processor!"

"Coming!" I called, reaching out for Tyler's hand. "You ready?"

He took it, standing and pulling me into his arms. "Remember when I said... life was like a hot air balloon? Every time we started gaining altitude, something would shoot us down?"

"Yeah." I put my arms around his neck.

"But you said it was like a roller coaster. With all these ups and downs..."

"Uh-huh." I cocked my head at him. "And...?"

"These past couple years... we've just been going up and up..." He slid his hands down to my lower back. "I'm afraid we're due for a crash."

"Shhh." I kissed him quiet, still amazed that every time we touched felt electric. "I'm buckled in. We all are. We'll be fine, no matter what."

"Mamamama!" The sound came from the room next to ours. Followed by, "Dadadada!"

"You or me?" I smiled, hearing our impatient son standing and rattling the side of his crib, calling for me, then for his father. Oliver was a towhead like his dad, but he had my little snub nose and, Tyler liked to say, "He inherited Katie's sass." Leanne often countered that with, "And his father's temper!"

"Both of us." Tyler gave me one more long, lingering kiss. "I love you, Katie. Up or down, it doesn't matter. As long as I've got you."

"Damn straight." I grinned, taking his hand as we headed toward the nursery. "I'm on the best ride of my life."

The End

ABOUT EMME ROLLINS

Emme Rollins is a NEW YORK TIMES bestselling author of New Adult/Mature Young Adult fiction. She's been writing since she could hold a crayon and still chews her pen caps to a mangled plastic mess. She did not, however, eat paste as a kid.

She has two degrees, a bachelor's and a master's, one of which she's still paying for, but neither of which she uses out in the "real world," because when she isn't writing, she spends her time growing an organic garden to feed her husband and children (and far too many rabbits and deer!) where they live on twenty gorgeous forested acres in rural Michigan.

She loves tending her beehives, keeping up with her daily yoga practice and going for long walks in the woods with her boxer, Rodeo, who loves chasing squirrels almost as much as Emme loves writing!

Emme loves hearing from fans, so feel free to contact her.

www.emmerollins.com

Join Emme's newsletter – get updates on new releases!
www.emmerollins.com/newsletter

DEAR ROCKSTAR
New-Adult Rock Star Romance

The best things in life are crazy...

Sara is obsessed with rock star Tyler Vincent, and as she works to complete her senior year, she's determined to find a way to meet him--although her best friend, Aimee, keeps telling her to find a different escape from her desperately violent home life.

Complications arise when Dale, the mysterious new transfer student, sets his sights on Sara, and she falls for this rock-star-in-the-making in spite of her better judgment. When Sara wins a contest, she is faced with a choice--travel to Tyler Vincent's home town to meet him, or stay and support Dale in a Battle-of-the-Bands hosted by MTV.

Their triangulated relationship is pushed to its breaking point, but there is another, deeper secret that Dale's been keeping that just may break things wide open...

Turn up your collar, feather your hair, and splash on some Polo, because we're going back to the '80's when MTV played music videos, there was no such thing as American Idol, and becoming a star meant doing nothing short of crazy for that one, big break.

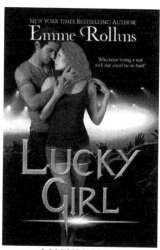

LUCKY GIRL
The SEQUEL to DEAR ROCKSTAR

Who knew loving a real rock star could be so hard?

Sara is Dale Diamond's biggest fan—and one of his biggest secrets. Catapulted to fame, Dale and his band, Black Diamond, are learning to deal with the grueling realities of the music business... including frenzied groupies. Dale's agent, determined to preserve the musician's image as a sexy single man, won't let fans know he has a girlfriend.

All Dale wants is to make music and love Sara. But he's caught up in the demands of recording and touring, while Sara has graduated art school and found a job. She and her rocker boyfriend are starting down different paths. Sara knows she's the luckiest girl in the world to have Dale in her life—but luck is about to run out.

A lurking, dark past will come back to haunt them both, forcing two young lovers to face harsh realities about life and each other. When the weight of the world is on their shoulders, will Dale and Sara be able to hold it all together for the sake of their love?

Made in the USA
Middletown, DE
07 February 2016